Christmas Eve
and
Christmas Day

Christmas Eve and Christmas Day

Ten Christmas Stories

EDWARD EVERETT HALE

PERUSE PRESS · LOS ANGELES

TITLE:
Christmas Eve and Christmas Day

SUBTITLE:
Ten Christmas Stories

AUTHOR:
Edward Everett Hale
1822–1909

EDITOR:
Mark Diederichsen

PUBLISHER:
Peruse Press
Los Angeles, California

FIRST PERUSE PRESS EDITION

FIRST PRINTING:
2013

FRONTISPIECE:
Felix Octavius Carr Darley
1822–1888
Daily Bread
1873
wood engraving

ISBN-TEN: 0615930743
ISBN-THIRTEEN: 978-0615930749

CONTENTS

PREFACE

This is a collection of ten Christmas Stories, some of which have been published before. I have added a little essay, written on the occasion of the first Christmas celebrated by the King of Italy in Rome.

The first story has never before been published.

It is but fair to say that I have not drawn on imagination for Laura's night duty, alone upon her island. This is simply the account of what a brave New-England woman did, under like circumstances, because it was the duty next her hand.

If any reader observes a resemblance between her position and that of a boy in another story in this volume, I must disarm censure, by saying, that she had never heard of him when she was called to this duty, and that I had never heard of her when I wrote his story.

— Edward Everett Hale

They Saw a Great Light

CHAPTER I

ANOTHER GENERATION

*H*ere he comes! here he comes!"

"He" was the "post-rider," an institution now almost of the past. He rode by the house and threw off a copy of the "Boston Gazette." Now the "Boston Gazette," of this particular issue, gave the results of the drawing of the great Massachusetts State Lottery of the Eastern Lands in the Waldo Patent.

Mr. Cutts, the elder, took the "Gazette," and opened it with a smile that pretended to be careless; but even he showed the eager anxiety which they all felt, as he tore off the wrapper and unfolded the fatal sheet. "Letter from London," "Letter from Philadelphia," "Child with two heads,"—thus he ran down the columns of the little page,—uneasily. "Here it is! here it is!—Drawing of the great State Lottery. 'In the presence of the Honourable Treasurer of the Commonwealth, and of their Honours the Commissioners of the Honourable Council,—was drawn yesterday, at the State House, the first distribution of numbers'—here are the numbers,—'First combination, 375–1. Second, 421–7. Third, 591–6. Fourth, 594–1. Fifth,' "—and here Mr. Cutts started off his feet,—" 'Fifth, 219–7.' Sybil, my darling! it is so! 219–7! See, dear child! 219–7! 219–7! O my God! to think it should come so!"

And he fairly sat down, and buried his head in his hands, and cried.

The others, for a full minute, did not dare break in on excitement so intense, and were silent; but, in a minute more, of course, little Simeon, the youngest of the tribes who were represented there, gained courage to pick up the paper, and to spell out again the same words which his father had read with so much emotion; and, with his sister Sally, who came to help him, to add to the store of information, as to what prize number 5—219–7—might bring.

For this was a lottery in which there were no blanks. The old Commonwealth of Massachusetts, having terrible war debts to pay after the Revolution, had nothing but lands in Maine to pay them with. Now lands in Maine were not very salable, and, if the simple and ordinary process of sale had been followed, the lands might not have been sold till this day. So they were distributed by these Lotteries, which in that time seemed gigantic. Every ticket-holder had some piece of land awarded to him, I think,—but to the most, I fear, the lands were hardly worth the hunting up, to settle upon. But, to induce as many to buy as might, there were prizes. No. 1, I think, even had a "stately mansion" on the land,—according to the advertisement. No. 2 had some special water-power facilities. No. 5, which Mr. Cutts's ticket had drawn, was two thousand acres on Tripp's Cove,—described in the programme as that "well-known Harbor of Refuge, where Fifty Line of Battle Ship could lie in safety." To this cove the two thousand acres so adjoined that the programme represented them as the site of the great "Mercantile Metropolis of the Future."

Samuel Cutts was too old a man, and had already tested too critically his own powers in what the world calls "business," by a sad satire, to give a great deal of faith to the promises of the prospectus, as to the commercial prosperity of Tripp's Cove. He had come out of the Revolution a Brigadier-General, with an honorable record of service,—with rheumatism which would never be cured,—with a good deal of paper money which would never be redeemed, which the Continent and the Commonwealth had paid him for his seven years,—and without that place in the world of peace which he had had when these years began. The very severest trial of the Revolution was to be found in the condition in which the officers of the army were left after it was over. They were men who had distinguished themselves in their profession, and who had done their very best to make that profession unnecessary in the future. To go back to their old callings was hard. Other men were in their places, and there did not seem to be room for two. Under the wretched political system of the old Confederation there was no such rapid spring of the material prosperity of the country as should find for them new fields in new enterprise. Peace did any thing but lead in Plenty. Often indeed, in history, has Plenty been a little coy before she could be tempted, with her pretty tender feet, to press the stubble and the ashes left by the havoc of War. And thus it was that General Cutts had returned to his old love whom he had married in a leave of absence just before Bunker Hill, and had begun his new life with her in Old Newbury in Massachusetts, at a time when there was little opening for him,—or for any man who had spent seven years in learning how to do well what was never to be done again.

And in doing what there was to do he had not succeeded. He had just squeezed pork and potatoes and Indian meal enough out of a worn-out farm to keep Sybil, his wife, and their growing family of children alive. He had, once or twice, gone up to Boston to find what chances might be open for him there. But, alas, Boston was in a bad way too, as well as Samuel Cutts. Once he had joined some old companions, who had gone out to the Western Reserve in Northern Ohio, to see what opening might be there. But the outlook seemed unfavorable for carrying so far, overland, a delicate woman and six little children into a wilderness. If he could have scraped together a little money, he said, he would buy a share in one of the ships he saw rotting in Boston or Salem, and try some foreign adventure. But, alas! the ships would not have been rotting had it been easy for any man to scrape together a little money to buy them. And so, year in and year out, Samuel Cutts and his wife dressed the children more and more plainly, bought less sugar and more molasses, brought down the family diet more strictly to pork and beans, pea-soup, hasty-pudding, and rye-and-indian,—and Samuel Cutts looked more and more sadly on the prospect before these boys and girls, and the life for which he was training them.

Do not think that he was a profligate, my dear cousin Eunice, because he had bought a lottery ticket. Please to observe that to buy lottery tickets was represented to be as much the duty of all good citizens, as it was proved to be, eleven years ago, your duty to make Havelocks and to knit stockings. Samuel Cutts, in the outset, had bought his lottery ticket only "to encourage the others," and to do his honorable share in paying the war debt. Then, I must confess, he had thought more of the ticket than he had supposed he would. The children had made a romance about it,—what they would do, and what they would not do, if they drew the first prize. Samuel Cutts and Sybil Cutts themselves had got drawn into the interest of the children, and many was the night when they had sat up, without any light but that of a pine-torch, planning out the details of the little colony they would form at the East-ward,—if—if only one of the ten great prizes should, by any marvel, fall to him. And now Tripp's Cove—which, perhaps, he had thought of as much as he had thought of any of the ten—had fallen to him. This was the reason why he showed so much emotion, and why he could hardly speak, when he read the numbers. It was because that had come to him which represented so completely what he wanted, and yet which he had not even dared to pray for. It was so much more than he expected,—it was the dream of years, indeed, made true.

For Samuel Cutts had proved to himself that he was a good leader of men. He knew he was, and many men knew it who had followed him under Carolina suns, and in the snows of Valley Forge. Samuel Cutts knew, equally well, that he was not a good maker of money, nor creator of pork and potatoes. Six years of farming in the valley of the Merrimac had proved that to him, if he had never learned it before. Samuel Cutts's dream had been, when he went away to explore the Western Reserve, that he would like to bring together some of the best line officers and some of the best privates of the old "Fighting Twenty-seventh," and take them, with his old provident skill, which had served them so well upon so many camping-grounds, to some region where they could stand by each other again, as they had stood by each other before, and where sky and earth would yield them more than sky and earth have yet yielded any man in

Eastern Massachusetts. Well! as I said, the Western Reserve did not seem to be the place. After all, "the Fighting Twenty-seventh" were not skilled in the tilling of the land. They furnished their quota when the boats were to be drawn through the ice of the Delaware, to assist in Rahl's Christmas party at Trenton. Many was the embarkation at the "head of Elk," in which the "Fighting Twenty-seventh" had provided half the seamen for the transport. It was "the Fighting Twenty-seventh" who cut out the "Princess Charlotte" cutter in Edisto Bay. But the "Fighting Twenty-seventh" had never, so far as any one knew, beaten one sword into one plough-share, nor one spear into one pruning-hook. But Tripp's Cove seemed to offer a different prospect. Why not, with a dozen or two of the old set, establish there, not the New Jerusalem, indeed, but something a little more elastic, a little more helpful, a little more alive, than these kiln-dried, sun-dried, and time-dried old towns of the seaboard of Massachusetts? At any rate, they could live together in Tripp's Cove, as they wintered together at Valley Forge, at Bennett's Hollow, by the Green Licks, and in the Lykens Intervale. This was the question which Samuel Cutts wanted to solve, and which the fatal figures 219-7 put him in the way of solving.

"Tripp's Cove is our Christmas present," said Sybil Cutts to her husband, as they went to bed. But so far removed were the habits of New England then from the observance of ecclesiastical anniversaries, that no one else had remembered that day that it was Christmas which was passing.

CHAPTER II

TRIPP'S COVE

C all this a long preface, if you please, but it seems to me best to tell this story so that I may explain what manner of people those were and are who lived, live, and will live, at Tripp's Cove,—and why they have been, are, and will be linked together, with a sort of family tie and relationship which one does not often see in the villages self-formed or formed at hap-hazard on the seaside, on the hillside, or in the prairies of America. Tripp's Cove never became "the Great Mercantile City of the Future," nor do I believe it ever will. But there Samuel Cutts lived in a happy life for fifty years,—and there he died, honored, blessed, and loved. By and by there came the second war with England,—the "Endymion" came cruising along upon the coast, and picking up the fishing-boats and the coasters, burning the ships on the stocks, or compelling the owners to ransom them. Old General Cutts was seventy years old then; but he was, as he had always been, the head of the settlement at Tripp's,—and there was no lack of men younger than he, the sergeants or the high-privates of the "Fighting Twenty-seventh," who drilled the boys of the village for whatever service might impend. When the boys went down to Runkin's and sent the "Endymion's" boats back to her with half their crews dead or dying, faster than they came, old General Cutts was with them, and took sight on his rifle as quickly and as bravely as the best of them. And so twenty years more passed on,—and, when he was well nigh ninety, the dear old man died full of years and full of blessings, all because he had launched out for himself, left the life he was not fit for, and undertaken life in which he was at home.

Yes! and because of this also, when 1861 came with its terrible alarm to the whole country, and its call to duty, all Tripp's Cove was all right. The girls were eager for service, and the boys were eager for service. The girls stood by the boys, and the boys stood by the girls. The husbands stood by the wives, and the wives stood by the husbands. I do not mean that there was not many another community in which everybody was steadfast and true. But I do mean that here was one great family, although the census rated it as five-and-twenty families,—which had one heart and one soul in the contest, and which went into it with one heart and one soul,—every man and every woman of them all bearing each other's burdens.

Little Sim Cutts, who broke the silence that night when the post-man threw down the "Boston Gazette," was an old man of eighty-five when they all got the news of the shots at Fort Sumter. The old man was as hale and hearty as are half the men of sixty in this land to-day. With all his heart he encouraged the boys who volunteered in answer to the first call for regiments from Maine. Then with full reliance on the traditions of the "Fighting Twenty-seventh," he explained to the fishermen and the coasters that Uncle Abraham would need them for his web-footed service, as well as for his legions on the land. And they found out their ways to Portsmouth and to Charlestown, so that they might enter the navy as their brothers entered the army. And so it was, that, when Christmas came in 1861, there was at Tripp's Cove only one of that noble set of young fellows, who but a year before was hauling hemlock and spruce and fir and pine at Christmas at the girls' order, and worked in the meeting-house for two days as the girls bade them work, so that when Parson Spaulding came in to preach his Christmas sermon, he thought the house was a bit of the woods themselves. Only one!

And who was he?

How did he dare stay among all those girls who were crying out their eyes, and sewing their fingers to the bones,—meeting every afternoon in one sitting-room or another, and devouring every word that came from the army? They read the worst-spelled letter that came home from Mike Sawin, and prized it and blessed it and cried over it, as heartily as the noblest description of battle that came from the pen of Carleton or of Swinton.

Who was he?

Ah! I have caught you, have I? That was Tom Cutts,—the old General's great-grandson,—Sim Cutts's grandson,—the very noblest and bravest of them all. He got off first of all. He had the luck to be at Bull Run,—and to be cut off from his regiment. He had the luck to hide under a corn crib, and to come into Washington whole, a week after the regiment. He was the first man in Maine, they said, to enlist for the three-years' service. Perhaps the same thing is said of many others. He had come home and raised a new company,—and he was making them fast into good soldiers, out beyond Fairfax Court-House. So that the Brigadier would do any thing Tom Cutts wanted. And when, on the first of December, there came up to the Major-General in command a request for leave of absence from Tom Cutts, respectfully referred to Colonel This, who had respectfully referred it to General That, who had respectfully referred it to Adjutant-General T'other,—all these dignitaries had respectfully recommended that the request be granted. For even in the sacred purlieux of the top Major-General's Head-quarters, it was understood that Cutts was going home for no less a purpose than the being married to the prettiest and sweetest and best girl in Eastern Maine.

Well! for my part I do not think that the aids and their informants were in the wrong about this. Surely that Christmas Eve, as Laura Marvel stood up with Tom Cutts in front of Parson Spaulding, in presence of what there was left of the Tripp's Cove community, I would have said that Laura was the loveliest bride I ever saw. She is tall; she is graceful; she has rather a startled look when you speak to her, suddenly or gently, but the startled look just bewitches you. Black hair,—she got that from the Italian blood in her grandmother's family,—exquisite blue eyes,—that is a charming combination with black hair,—perfect teeth,—and matchless color,—and she had it all, when she was married,—she was a blushing bride and not a fainting one. But then what stuff this is,—nobody knew he cared a straw for Laura's hair or her cheek,—it was that she looked "just lovely," and that she was "just lovely,"—so self-forgetful in all her ways, after that first start,—so eager to know just where she could help, and so determined to help just there. Why! she led all the girls in the village, when she was only fourteen, because they loved her so. She was the one who made the rafts when there was a freshet,—and took them all out together on the mill-pond. And, when the war came, she was of course captain of the girl's sewing,—she packed the cans of pickles and fruit for the Sanitary,—she corresponded with the State Adjutant:—heavens! from morning to night, everybody in the village ran to Laura,—not because she was the prettiest creature you ever looked upon,—but because she was the kindest, truest, most loyal, and most helpful creature that ever lived,—be the same man or woman.

Now had you rather be named Laura Cutts or Laura Marvel? Marvel is a good name,—a weird, miraculous sort of name. Cutts is not much of a name. But Laura had made up her mind to be Laura Cutts after Tom had asked her about it,—and here they are standing before dear old Parson Spaulding, to receive his exhortation,—and to be made one before God and man.

Dear Laura! How she had laughed with the other girls, all in a good-natured way, at the good Parson's exhortation to the young couples. Laura had heard it twenty times,—for she had "stood up" with twenty of the girls, who had dared The Enterprise of Life before her! Nay, Laura could repeat, with all the emphasis, the most pathetic passage of the whole,—"And above all,—my beloved young friends,—first of all and last of all,—let me beseech you as you climb the hill of life together, hand with hand, and step with step,—that you will look beyond the crests upon its summit to the eternal lights which blaze in the infinite heaven of the Better Land beyond." Twenty times had Laura heard this passage,—nay, ten times, I am afraid, had she, in an honest and friendly way, repeated it, under strict vows of secrecy, to the edification of circles of screaming girls. But now the dear child looked truly and loyally into the old man's face, as he went on from word to word, and only thought of him, and of how noble and true he was,—and of the Great Master whom he represented there,—and it was just as real to her and to Tom Cutts that they must look into the Heaven of heavens for life and strength, as Parson Spaulding wanted it to be. When he prayed with all his heart, she prayed; what he hoped, she hoped; what he promised for her, she promised to her Father in heaven; and what he asked her to promise by word aloud, she promised loyally and eternally.

And Tom Cutts? He looked so handsome in his uniform,—and he looked like the man he was. And in those days, the uniform, if it were only a flannel fatigue-jacket on a private's back, was as beautiful as the flag; nothing more beautiful than either for eyes to look upon.

And when Parson Spaulding had said the benediction, and the Amen,—and when he had kissed Laura, with her eyes full of tears,—and when he had given Tom Cutts joy,—then all the people came up in a double line,—and they all kissed Laura,—and they shook hands with Tom as if they would shake his hands off,—and in the half-reticent methods of Tripp's Cove, every lord and lady bright that was in Moses Marvel's parlor there, said, "honored be the bravest knight, beloved the fairest fair."

And there was a bunch of laurel hanging in the middle of the room, as make-believe mistletoe. And the boys, who could not make believe even that they were eighteen, so that they had been left at home, would catch

Phebe, and Sarah, and Mattie, and Helen, when by accident they crossed underneath the laurel,—and would kiss them, for all their screaming. And soon Moses Marvel brought in a waiter with wedding-cake, and Nathan Philbrick brought in a waiter with bride-cake, and pretty Mattie Marvel brought in a waiter with currant wine. And Tom Cutts gave every girl a piece of wedding-cake himself, and made her promise to sleep on it. And before they were all gone, he and Laura had been made to write names for the girls to dream upon, that they might draw their fortunes the next morning. And before long Moses Cutts led Mrs. Spaulding out into the great family-room, and there was the real wedding supper. And after they had eaten the supper, Bengel's fiddle sounded in the parlor, and they danced, and they waltzed, and they polkaed to their hearts' content. And so they celebrated the Christmas of 1861.

Too bad! was not it? Tom's leave was only twenty days. It took five to come. It took five to go. After the wedding there were but seven little days. And then he kissed dear Laura good-by,—with tears running from his eyes and hers,—and she begged him to be sure she should be all right, and he begged her to be certain nothing would happen to him. And so, for near two years, they did not see each other's faces again.

Christmas Eve again!

Moses Marvel has driven out his own bays in his own double cutter to meet the stage at Fordyce's. On the back seat is Mattie Marvel, with a rosy little baby all wrapped up in furs, who has never seen his father. Where is Laura?

"Here she comes! here she comes!" Sure enough! Here is the stage at last. Job Stiles never swept round with a more knowing sweep, or better satisfied with his precious freight at Fordyce's, than he did this afternoon. And the curtains were up already. And there is Laura, and there is Tom! He is pale, poor fellow. But how pleased he is! Laura is out first, of course. And then she gives him her hand so gently, and the others all help. And here is the hero at Marvel's side, and he is bending over his baby, whom he does not try to lift with his one arm,—and Mattie is crying, and I believe old Moses Marvel is crying,—but everybody is as happy as a king, and everybody is talking at one time,—and all the combination has turned out well.

Tom Cutts had had a hole made through his left thigh, so that they despaired of his life. And, as he lay on the ground, a bit of a shell had struck his left forearm and knocked that to pieces. Tom Cutts had been sent back to hospital at Washington, and reported by telegraph as mortally wounded. But almost as soon as Tom Cutts got to the Lincoln Hospital himself, Laura Cutts got there too, and then Tom did not mean to die if he could help it, and Laura did not mean to have him. And the honest fellow held to his purpose in that steadfast Cutts way. The blood tells, I believe. And love tells. And will tells. How much love has to do with will! "I believe you are a witch, Mrs. Cutts," the doctor used to say to her. "Nothing but good happens to this good-man of yours." Bits of bone came out just as they were wanted to. Inflammation kept away just as it was told to do. And the two wounds ran a race with each other in healing after their fashion. "It will be a beautiful stump after all," said the doctor, where poor Laura saw little beauty. But every thing was beautiful to her, when at last he told her that she might wrap her husband up as well as she knew how, and take him home and nurse him there. So she had telegraphed that they were coming, and that was the way in which it happened that her father and her sister had brought out the baby to meet them both at Fordyce's. Mattie's surprise had worked perfectly.

And now it was time for Laura's surprise!

After she had her baby in her own arms, and was on the back seat of the sleigh; after Tom was well wrapped up by her side, with his well arm just supporting the little fellow's head; after Mattie was all tucked in by her father, and Mr. Marvel himself had looked round to say, "All ready?" then was it that Jem Marvel first stepped out from the stage, and said, "Haven't you one word for me, Mattie?" Then how they screamed again! For everybody thought Jem was in the West Indies. He was cruising there, on board the "Greywing," looking after blockaders who took the Southern route. Nobody dreamed of Jem's being at Christmas. And here he had stumbled on Tom and Laura in the New Haven train as they came on! Jem had been sent into New York with a prize. He had got leave, and was on his way to see the rest of them. He had bidden Laura not say one word, and so he had watched one greeting from the stage, before he broke in to take his part for another.

Oh! what an uproarious Christmas that was when they all came home! No! Tom Cutts would not let one of them be sad! He was the cheeriest of them all. He monopolized the baby, and showed immense power in the way of baby talk and of tending. Laura had only to sit on the side of the room and be perfectly happy. It was very soon known what the arrivals were. And Parson Spaulding came in, and his wife. Of course the Cuttses had been there already. Then everybody came. That is the simplest way of putting it. They all would have wanted to come, because in that community there was not one person who did not love Laura and Tom and Jem. But whether they would have come, on the very first night, I am not sure. But this was Christmas Eve, and the girls were finishing off the meeting-house just as the stage and the sleigh came in. And, in a minute, the news was everywhere. And, of course, everybody felt he might just go in to get news from the fleet or the army. Nor was there one household in Tripp's Cove which was not more or less closely represented in the fleet or the army. So there was really, as the evening passed, a town-meeting in Moses Marvel's sitting-room and parlor; and whether Moses Marvel were most pleased, or Mrs. Marvel, or Laura,—who sat and beamed,—or old General Simeon Cutts, I am sure I do not know.

That was indeed a merry Christmas!

But after that I must own it was hard sledding for Tom Cutts and for pretty Laura. A hero with one blue sleeve pinned neatly together, who, at the best, limps as he walks, quickens all your compassion and gratitude;—yes! But when you are selecting a director of your lumber works, or when you are sending to New York to buy goods, or when you are driving a line of railway through the wilderness, I am afraid you do not choose that hero to do your work for you. Or if you do, you were not standing by when Tom Cutts was looking right and looking left for something to do, so that he might keep the wolf from the door. It was sadly like the life that his great-grandfather, Samuel Cutts, led at the old farm in old Newbury after the old war. Tom lost his place when he went to the front, and he could not find it again.

Laura, sweet girl, never complained. No, nor Moses Marvel. He never complained, nor would he complain if Tom and his wife and children had lived with him till doomsday. "Good luck for us," said Moses Marvel, and those were many words for him to say in one sentence. But Tom was proud, and it ground him to the dust to be eating Moses Marvel's bread when he had not earned it, and to have nothing but his major's pension to buy Laura and the babies their clothes with, and to keep the pot a-boiling.

Of course Jem joined the fleet again. Nor did Jem return again till the war was over. Then he came, and came with prize-money. He and Tom had many talks of going into business together, with Tom's brains and Jem's money. But nothing came of this. The land was no place for Jem. He was a regular Norse man, as are almost all of the Tripp's Cove boys who have come from the loins of the "Fighting Twenty-seventh." They sniff the tempest from afar off; and when they hear of Puget Sound, or of Alaska, or of Wilkes's Antarctic Continent, they fancy that they hear a voice from some long-lost home, from which they have strayed away. And so Laura knew, and Tom knew, that any plans which rested on Jem's staying ashore were plans which had one false element in them. The raven would be calling him, and it might be best, once for all, to let him follow the raven till the raven called no more.

So Jem put his prize-money into a new bark, which he found building at Bath; and they called the bark the "Laura," and Tom and Laura Cutts went to the launching, and Jem superintended the rigging of her himself; and then he took Tom and Laura and the babies with him to New York, and a high time they had together there. Tom saw many of the old army boys, and Laura hunted up one or two old school friends; and they saw Booth in Iago, and screamed themselves hoarse at Niblo's, and heard Rudolphsen and Johannsen in the German opera; they rode in the Park, and they walked in the Park; they browsed in the Astor and went shopping at Stewart's, and saw the people paint porcelain at Haighwout's; and, by Mr. Alden's kindness, went through the wonders of Harper's. In short, for three weeks, all of which time they lived on board ship, they saw the lions of New York as children of the public do, for whom that great city decks itself and prepares its wonders, albeit their existence is hardly known to its inhabitants.

Meanwhile Jem had chartered the "Laura" for a voyage to San Francisco. And so, before long, her cargo began to come on board; and she and Tom and the babies took a mournful farewell, and came back to Tripp's Cove again, to Moses Marvel's house. And poor Tom thought it looked smaller than ever, and that he should find it harder than ever to settle down to being of no use to anybody, and to eat Moses Marvel's bread,—without house or barn, or bin or oven, or board or bed, even the meanest, of his own. Poor Tom! and this was the reward of being the first man in Maine to enter for three years!

And then things went worse and worse. Moses Marvel was as good and as taciturn as ever. But Moses Marvel's affairs did not run as smoothly as he liked. Moses held on, upon one year's cutting of lumber, perfectly determined that lumber should rise, because it ought to; and Moses paid very high usury on the money he borrowed, because he would hold on. Moses was set in his way,—like other persons whom you and I know,—and to this lumber he held and held, till finally the bank would not renew his notes. No; and they would not discount a cent for him at Bangor, and Moses came back from a long, taciturn journey he had started on in search of money, without any money; and with only the certainty that if he did not mean to have the sheriff sell his lumber, he must sell it for himself. Nay! he must sell it before the fourth of the next month, and for cash; and must sell at the very bottom of a long falling market! Poor Moses Marvel! That operation served to show that he joined all the Cutts want of luck with the Marvel obstinacy. It was a wretched twelvemonth, the whole of it; and it made that household, and made Tom Cutts, more miserable and more.

Then they became anxious about the "Laura," and Jem. She made almost a clipper voyage to California. She discharged her cargo in perfect order. Jem made a capital charter for Australia and England, and knew that from England it would be easy to get a voyage home. He sailed from California, and then the letters stopped. No! Laura dear, no need in reading every word of the ship-news in the "Semi-weekly Advertiser;" the name of your namesake is not there. Eight, nine, ten months have gone by, and there is no port in Christendom which has seen Jem's face, or the Laura's private signal. Do not strain your eyes over the "Semi-weekly" more.

No! dear Laura's eyes will be dimmed by other cares than the ship-news. Tom's father, who had shared Tom's wretchedness, and would gladly have had them at his home, but that Moses Marvel's was the larger and the less peopled of the two,—Tom's father was brought home speechless one day, by the men who found him where he had fallen on the road, his yoke of oxen not far away, waiting for the voice which they were never to hear again. Whether he had fallen from the cart, in some lurch it made, and broken his spine, or whether all this distress had brought on of a sudden a stroke of paralysis, so that he lost his consciousness before he fell, I do not know. Nor do I see that it matters much, though the chimney-corners of Tripp's Cove discuss the question quite eagerly to this hour. He lay there month after month, really unconscious. He smiled gently when they brought him food. He tried to say "Thank you," they thought, but he did not speak to the wife of his bosom, who had been the Laura Marvel of her day, in any different way from that in which he tried to speak to any stranger of them all. A living death he lay in as those tedious months went by.

Yet my dear Laura was as cheerful, and hopeful, and buoyant as ever. Tom Cutts himself was ashamed to brood when he got a sight of her. Mother Cutts herself would lie down and rest herself when Laura came round, with the two children, as she did every afternoon. Moses Marvel himself was less taciturn when Laura put the boys, one at one side, one at the other, of his chair, at the tea-table. And in both of those broken households, from one end to the other, they knew the magic of dear Laura's spells. So that when this Christmas came, after poor Mr. Cutts had been lying senseless so long,—when dear Laura bade them all take hold and fit up a Christmas-tree, with all the adornments, for the little boys, and for the Spaulding children, and the Marvel cousins, and the Hopkinses, and the Tredgolds, and the Newmarch children,—they all obeyed her loyally, and without wondering. They obeyed her, with her own determination that they would have one merry Christmas more. It seems a strange thing to people who grew up outside of New England. But this was the first Christmas tree ever seen at Tripp's Cove, for all such festivities are of recent importation in such regions. But there was something for every child. They heaped on more wood, and they kept a merry Christmas despite the storm without. This was Laura's will, and Laura had her way.

And she had her reward. Job Stiles came round to the door, when he had put up his horses, and called Tom out, and gave him a letter which he had brought from Ellsworth. And Tom read the letter, and he called Laura to read it. And Laura left the children, and sat at the kitchen table with him and read it, and said, "Thank God! this is a Christmas present indeed. Could any thing in this world be better?"

This is the letter:—

JOHN WILDAIR TO TOM CUTTS

Dear Tom,—I am just back from Washington. I have seen them all, and have done my best, and have failed. They say and I believe that the collectorship was promised to Waters before the old man's death,—that Waters had honest claims,—he has but one leg, you know,—and that it must go to him. As for the surveyorship, the gift of that is with Plumptre. And you know that I might as well ask the Pope to give me any thing as he. And if he hates anybody more than me, why it is your wife's father. So I could do nothing there.

Let me say this, though it seems nothing. If, while we are waiting to look round, you like to take the Bell and Hammer Light-house, you may have the place to-morrow. Of course I know it is exile in winter. But in summer it is lovely. You have your house, your stores, two men under you (they are double lights), and a thousand dollars. I have made them promise to give it to no one till they hear from me. Though I know you ought not take any such place, I would not refuse it till I let you know. I send this to Ellsworth for the stage-driver to take, and you must send your answer by special messenger, that I may telegraph to Washington at once.

I am very sorry, dear Tom, to have failed you so. But I did my best, you know. Merry Christmas to Laura and the babies.

TRULY YOURS,

— JOHN WILDAIR
PORTLAND, DEC. 24, 1868

That was Laura and Tom's Christmas present. An appointment as light-house keeper, with a thousand a year!

But even if they had made Tom a turnpike keeper, they would not have made Laura a misanthrope. He, poor fellow, gladly accepted the appointment. She, sweet creature, as gladly accepted her part of it. Early March saw them on the Bell and Hammer. April saw the early flowers come,—and May saw Laura with both her babies on the beach, laughing at them as they wet their feet,—digging holes in the sand for them,—and sending the bigger boy to run and put salt upon the tails of the peeps as they ran along the shore. And Tom Cutts, when his glass was clear to his mind, and the reflectors polished to meet even his criticism, would come down and hunt up Laura and the children. And when she had put the babies to sleep, old Mipples, who was another of the descendants of the "Fighting Twenty-seventh," would say, "Just you go out with the Major, mum, and if they wake up and I can't still them, I'll blow the horn." Not that he ever did blow the horn. All the more certain was Laura that she could tramp over the whole island with Tom Cutts, or she could sit and knit or sew, and Tom could read to her, and these days were the happiest days of her married life, and brought back the old sunny days of the times before Fort Sumter again. Ah me! if such days of summer and such days of autumn would last forever!

But they will not last forever. November came, and the little colony went into winter quarters. December came. And we were all double-banked with sea-weed. The stoves were set up in-doors. The double doors were put on outside, and we were all ready for the "Osprey." The "Osprey" was the Government steamer which was to bring us our supplies for the winter, chiefly of colza oil,—and perhaps some coal. But the "Osprey" does not appear. December is half gone, and no "Osprey." We can put the stoves on short allowance, but not our two lanterns. They will only run to the 31st of January, the nights are so long, if the "Osprey" does not come before then.

That is our condition, when old Mipples, bringing back the mail, brings a letter from Boston to say that the "Osprey" has broken her main-shaft, and may not be repaired before the 15th of January,—that Mr. Cutts, will therefore, if he needs oil, take an early opportunity to supply himself from the light at Squire's,—and that an order on the keeper at Squire's is enclosed.

To bring a cask of oil from Squire's is no difficult task to a Tripp's Cove man. It would be no easy one, dear reader, to you and me. Squire's is on the mainland,—our nearest neighbor at the Bell and Hammer,—it revolves once a minute, and we watch it every night in the horizon. Tom waited day by day for a fine day,—would not have gone for his oil indeed till the New Year came in, but that Jotham Fields, the other assistant, came down with a fever turn wholly beyond Laura's management, and she begged Tom to take the first fine day to carry him to a doctor. To bring a doctor to him was out of the question.

"And what will you do?" said Tom.

"Do? I will wait till you come home. Start any fine day after you have wound up the lights on the last beat,—take poor Jotham to his mother's house,—and if you want you may bring back your oil. I shall get along with the children very well,—and I will have your dinner hot when you come home."

Tom doubted. But the next day Jotham was worse. Mipples voted for carrying him ashore, and Laura had her way. The easier did she have it, because the south wind blew softly, and it was clear to all men that the run could be made to Squire's in a short two hours. Tom finally agreed to start early the next morning. He would not leave his sick man at his mother's, but at Squire's, and the people there could put him home. The weather was perfect, and an hour before daylight they were gone. They were all gone,— all three had to go. Mipples could not handle the boat alone, nor could Tom; far less could one of them manage the boat, take the oil, and see to poor Jotham also. Wise or not, this was the plan.

An hour before daylight they were gone. Half an hour after sunrise they were at Squire's. But the sun had risen red, and had plumped into a cloud. Before Jotham was carried up the cliff the wind was northwest, and the air was white with snow. You could not see the house from the boat, nor the boat from the house. You could not see the foremast of the boat from your seat in the stern-sheets, the air was so white with snow. They carried Jotham up. But they told John Wilkes, the keeper at Squire's, that they would come for the oil another day. They hurried down the path to the boat again, pushed her off, and headed her to the northeast determined not to lose a moment in beating back to the Bell and Hammer. Who would have thought the wind would haul back so without a sign of warning?

"Will it hold up, Simon?" said Tom to Mipples, wishing he might say something encouraging.

And all Simon Mipples would say was,—

"God grant it may!"

———————————

And Laura saw the sun rise red and burning. And Laura went up into the tower next the house, and put out the light there. Then she left the children in their cribs, and charged the little boy not to leave till she came back, and ran down to the door to go and put out the other light,—and as she opened it the blinding snow dashed in her face. She had not dreamed of snow before. But her water-proof was on, she pulled on her boots, ran quickly along the path to the other light, two hundred yards perhaps, climbed the stairway and extinguished that, and was at home again before the babies missed her.

For an hour or two Laura occupied herself with her household cares, and pretended to herself that she thought this was only a snow flurry that would soon clear away. But by the time it was ten o'clock she knew it was a stiff north-wester, and that her husband and Mipples were caught on shore. Yes, and she was caught with her babies alone on the island. Wind almost dead ahead to a boat from Squire's too, if that made any difference. That crossed

Laura's mind. Still she would not brood. Nay, she did not brood, which was much better than saying she would not brood. It crossed her mind that it was the day before Christmas, and that the girls at Tripp's were dressing the meeting-house for dear old Parson Spaulding. And then there crossed her mind the dear old man's speech at all weddings, "As you climb the hill of life together, my dear young friends," and poor Laura, as she kissed the baby once again, had courage to repeat it all aloud to her and her brother, to the infinite amazement of them both. They opened their great eyes to the widest as Laura did so. Nay, Laura had the heart to take a hatchet, and work out to leeward of the house, into a little hollow behind the hill, and cut up a savin bush from the thicket, and bring that in, and work for an hour over the leaves so as to make an evergreen frame to hang about General Cutts's picture. She did this that Tom might see she was not frightened when he got home.

When he got home! Poor girl! at the very bottom of her heart was the other and real anxiety,—*if* he got home. Laura knew Tom, of course, better than he knew himself, and she knew old Mipples too. So she knew, as well as she knew that she was rubbing black lead on the stove, while she thought these things over,—she knew that they would not stay at Squire's two minutes after they had landed Jotham Fields. She knew they would do just what they did,—put to sea, though it blew guns, though now the surf was running its worst on the Seal's Back. She knew, too, that if they had not missed the island, they would have been here, at the latest, before eleven o'clock. And by the time it was one she could no longer doubt that they had lost the island, and were tacking about looking for it in the bay, if, indeed, in that gale they dared to tack at all. No! Laura knew only too well, that where they were was beyond her guessing; that the good God and they two only knew.

"Come here, Tom, and let me tell you a story! Once there was a little boy, and he had two kittens. And he named one kitten Muff, and he named one kitten Buff!"—

Whang!

What was that?

"Tom, darling, take care of baby; do not let her get out of the cradle, while mamma goes to the door." Downstairs to the door. The gale has doubled its rage. How ever did it get in behind the storm-door outside? That "*whang*" was the blow with which the door, wrenched off its hinges, was flung against the side of the wood-house. Nothing can be done but to bolt the storm-door to the other passage, and bolt the outer window shutters, and then go back to the children.

"Once there was a little boy, and he had two kittens, and he named one Minna, and one Brenda"—

"No, mamma, no! one Muff, and one"—

"Oh, yes! my darling! once there was a little boy, and he had two kittens, and he named one Buff, and one Muff. And one day he went to walk"—

Heavens! the lanterns! Who was to trim the lamps? Strange to say, because this was wholly out of her daily routine, the men always caring for it of course, Laura had not once thought of it till now. And now it was after one o'clock. But now she did think of it with a will. "Come, Tommy, come and help mamma." And she bundled him up in his thickest storm rig. "Come up into the lantern." Here the boy had never come before. He was never frightened when he was with her. Else he might well have been frightened. And he was amazed there in the whiteness; drifts of white snow on the lee-side and the weather-side; clouds of white snow on the south-west sides and north-east sides; snow; snow everywhere; nothing but whiteness wherever he looked round.

Laura made short shift of those wicks which had burned all through the night before. But she had them ready. She wound up the carcels for their night's work. Again and again she drew her oil and filled up her reservoirs. And as she did so, an old text came on her, and she wondered whether Father Spaulding knew how good a text it would be for Christmas. And the fancy touched her, poor child, and as she led little Tom down into the nursery again, she could not help opening into the Bible Parson Spaulding gave her and reading:—

"'But the wise took oil in their vessels with their lamps. While the bridegroom tarried, they all slumbered and slept.' Dear Tommy, dear Tommy, my own child, we will not sleep, will we? 'While the bridegroom tarried,' O my dear Father in Heaven, let him come. 'And at midnight there was a cry made, Behold, the bridegroom cometh, go ye out to meet him;'" and she devoured little Tommy with kisses, and cried, "We will go, my darling, we will go, if he comes at the first hour,—or the second,—or the third! But now Tommy must come with mamma, and make ready for his coming." For there were the other lamps to trim in the other tower, with that heavy reach of snow between. And she did not dare leave the active boy alone in the house. Little Matty could be caged in her crib, and, even if she woke, she would at best only cry. But Tom was irrepressible.

So they unbolted the lee-door, and worked out into the snow. Then poor Laura, with the child, crept round into the storm. Heavens! how it raged and howled! Where was her poor bridegroom now? She seized up Tom, and turned her back to the wind, and worked along, go,—step sideway, sideway, the only way she could by step,—did it ever seem so far before? Tommy was crying. "One minute more, dear boy. Tommy shall see the other lantern. And Tommy shall carry mamma's great scissors up the stairs. Don't cry, my darling, don't cry."

Here is the door;—just as she began to wonder if she were dreaming or crazy. Not so badly drifted in as she feared. At least she is under cover.

"Up-a-day, my darling, up-a-day. One, two, what a many steps for Tommy! That's my brave boy." And they were on the lantern deck again, fairly rocking in the gale,—and Laura was chopping away on her stiff wicks, and pumping up her oil again, and filling the receivers, as if she had ever done it till this Christmas before. And she kept saying over to herself,—

"Then those virgins arose and trimmed their lamps."

"And I will light them," said she aloud. "That will save another walk at sundown. And I know these carcels run at least five hours." So she struck a match, and with some little difficulty coaxed the fibres to take fire. The yellow light flared luridly on the white snow-flakes, and yet it dazzled her and Tommy as it flashed on them from the reflectors. "Will anybody see it, mamma?" said the child. "Will papa see it?" And just then the witching devil who manages the fibres of memory, drew from the little crypt in Laura's brain, where they had been stored unnoticed years upon years, four lines of Leigh Hunt's, and the child saw that she was Hero:—

> "Then at the flame a torch of fire she lit,
>   And, o'er her head anxiously holding it,
>   Ascended to the roof, and, leaning there,
>   Lifted its light into the darksome air."

If only the devil would have been satisfied with this. But of course she could not remember that, without remembering Schiller:—

> "In the gale her torch is blasted,
>   Beacon of the hoped-for strand:
>   Horror broods above the waters,
>   Horror broods above the land."

And she said aloud to the boy, "Our torch shall not go out, Tommy,—come down, come down, darling, with mamma." But all through the day horrid lines from the same poem came back to her. Why did she ever learn it!

Why, but because dear Tom gave her the book himself; and this was his own version, as he sent it to her from the camp in the valley,—

> "Yes, 'tis he! although he perished,
>   Still his sacred troth he cherished."

"Why did Tom write it for me?"

> "And they trickle, lightly playing
>   O'er a corpse upon the sand."

"What a fool I am! Come, Tommy. Come, Matty, my darling. Mamma will tell you a story. Once there was a little boy, and he had two kittens. And he named one Buff and one Muff"— But this could not last for ever. Sundown came. And then Laura and Tommy climbed their own tower,— and she lighted her own lantern, as she called it. Sickly and sad through the storm, she could see the sister lantern burning bravely. And that was all she could see in the sullen whiteness. "Now, Tommy, my darling, we will come and have some supper." "And while the bridegroom tarried, they all slumbered and slept." "Yes, 'tis he; although he perished, still his sacred troth he cherished." "Come, Tommy,—come Tommy,—come, Tommy, let me tell you a story."

But the children had their supper,—asking terrible questions about papa,—questions which who should answer? But she could busy herself about giving them their oatmeal, and treating them to ginger-snaps, because it was Christmas Eve. Nay, she kept her courage, when Tommy asked if Santa Claus would come in the boat with papa. She fairly loitered over the undressing them. Little witches, how pretty they were in their flannel nightgowns! And Tommy kissed her, and gave her—ah me!—one more kiss for papa. And in two minutes they were asleep. It would have been better if they could have kept awake one minute longer. Now she was really alone. And very soon seven o'clock has come. She does not dare leave the clock-work at the outer lantern a minute longer. Tom and Mipples wind the works every four hours, and now they have run five. One more look at her darlings. Shall she ever see them again in this world? Now to the duty next her hand!

Yes, the wind is as fierce as ever! A point more to the north, Laura notices. She has no child to carry now. She tumbles once in the drift. But Laura has rolled in snow before. The pile at the door is three feet thick. But she works down to the latch,—and even her poor numb hand conquers it,—and it gives way. How nice and warm the tower is! and how well the lights burn! Can they be of any use this night to anybody? O my God, grant that they be of use to him!

She has wound them now. She has floundered into the snow again. Two or three falls on her way home,—but no danger that she loses the line of march. The light above her own house is before her. So she has only to aim at that. Home again! And now to wait for five hours,—and then to wind that light again—at midnight!

"And at midnight there was a cry made"—"oh dear!—if he would come,—I would not ask for any cry!"—

And Laura got down her choice inlaid box, that Jem brought her from sea,—and which held her treasures of treasures. And the dear girl did the best thing she could have done. She took these treasures out.—You know what they were, do not you? They were every letter Tom Cutts ever wrote her—from the first boy note in print,—"Laura,—these hedgehog quills are for you. I killed him. Tom." And Laura opened them all,—and read them one by one, each twice,—and put them back, in their order, without folding, into the box. At ten she stopped,—and worked her way upstairs into her own lantern,—and wound its works again. She tried to persuade herself that there was less wind,—did persuade herself so. But the snow was as steady as ever. Down the tower-stairs again,—and then a few blessed minutes brooding over Matty's crib, and dear little Tom who has kicked himself right athwart her own bed where she had laid him. Darlings! they are so lovely, their father must come home to see them! Back then to her kitchen fire. There are more of dear Tom's letters yet. How manly they are,—and how womanly. She will read them all!—will she ever dare to read them all again?

Yes,—she reads them all,—each one twice over,—and his soldier diary,—which John Wildair saved and sent home, and, as she lays it down, the clock strikes twelve. Christmas day is born!—

"And at midnight there was a cry made, Behold, the bridegroom cometh." Laura fairly repeated this aloud. She knew that the other carcel must be wound again. She dressed herself for the fight thoroughly. She ran in and trusted herself to kiss the children. She opened the lee-door again, and crept round again into the storm,—familiar now with such adventure. Did the surf beat as fiercely on the rocks? Surely not. But then the tide is now so low! So she came to her other tower, crept up and wound her clock-work up again, wiped off, or tried to wipe off, what she thought was mist gathering on the glasses, groped down the stairway, and looked up on the steady light above her own home. And the Christmas text came back to her. "The star went before them, and stood above the place where the young child was."

"A light to lighten the Gentiles,—and the glory of my people Israel!"

"By the way of the sea,"—and this Laura almost shouted aloud,—"Galilee of the Gentiles, the people who sat in darkness saw a great light, and to them who sat in the region and shadow of death light is sprung up." "Grant it, merciful Father,—grant it for these poor children!" And she almost ran through the heavy drifts, till she found the shelter again of her friendly tower. Her darlings had not turned in their bed, since she left them there.

And after this Laura was at rest. She took down her Bible, and read the Christmas chapters. It was as if she had never known before what darkness was,—or what the Light was, when it came. She took her Hymn Book and read all the Christmas Hymns. She took her Keble,—and read every poem for Advent and the hymn for Christmas morning. She knew this by heart long ago. Then she took Bishop Ken's "Christian Year,"—which Tom had given for her last birthday present,—and set herself bravely to committing his "Christmas Day" to memory:—

> "Celestial harps, prepare
>   To sound your loftiest air;
> You choral angels at the throne,
> Your customary hymns postpone;"

and thus, dear girl, she kept herself from thinking even of the wretched Hero and Leander lines, till her clock struck three. Upstairs then to her own tower, and to look out upon the night. The sister flame was steady. The wind was all hushed. But the snow was as steady, right and left, behind and before. Down again, one more look at the darlings, and then, as she walked up and down her little kitchen, she repeated the verses she had learned, and then sat down to—

> "You with your heavenly ray
> Gild the expanse this day;

> "You with your heavenly ray
> Gild—the expanse—this day;

> "You—with—your—heavenly—ray"—

Dear Laura, bless God, she is asleep. "He giveth his beloved sleep."

———————————

Her head is thrown back on the projecting wing of grandmamma's tall easy-chair, her arms are resting relaxed on its comfortable arms, her lips just open with a smile, as she dreams of something in the kingdom of God's heaven, when, as the lazy day just begins to grow gray, Tom, white with snow to his middle, holding the boat's lantern before him as he steals into her kitchen, crosses the room, and looks down on her,—what a shame to wake her,—bends down and kisses her!

Dear child! How she started,—"At midnight there is a cry made, Behold, the bridegroom cometh,"—"Why, Tom! Oh! my dearest, is it you?"

———————————

"Have I been asleep on duty?" This was her first word when she came fairly to herself.

"Guess not," said old Mipples, "both lanterns was burning when I come in. 'Most time to put 'em out, Major! 'Keepers must be diligent to save oil by all reasonable prevision.'"

"Is the north light burning?" said poor Laura. And she looked guiltily at her tell-tale clock.

"Darling," said Tom, reverently, "if it were not burning, we should not be here."

And Laura took her husband to see the babies, not willing to let his hand leave hers, nor he, indeed, to let hers leave his. Old Mipples thought himself one too many, and went away, wiping his eyes, to the other light. "Time to extinguish it," he said.

But before Tom and Laura had known he was gone, say in half an hour, that is, he was back again, hailing them from below.

"Major! Major! Major! An English steamer is at anchor in the cove, and is sending her boat ashore."

Tom and Laura rushed to the window; the snow was all over now, and they could see the monster lying within half a mile. "Where would they be, Miss Cutts, if somebody had not wound up the lamps at midnight? Guess they said 'Merry Christmas' when they see 'em." And Laura held her breath when she thought what might have been. Tom and Mipples ran down to the beach to hail them, and direct the landing. Tom and Mipples shook the hand of each man as he came ashore, and then Laura could see them hurrying to the house together. Steps on the landing; steps on the stairway,—the door is open, and,—not Tom this time,—but her dear lost brother Jem, in the flesh, and in a heavy pea-coat.

"Merry Christmas! Laura!"

———————————

"Laura," said Jem, as they sat at their Christmas dinner, "what do you think I thought of first, when I heard the cable run out so like blazes; when I rushed up and saw your yellow lanterns there?"

"How should I know, Jem?"

"'They that dwell in the shadow of death, upon them the light hath shined.'"

"But I did not think it was you, Laura."

Christmas Waits in Boston

CHAPTER I

I ALWAYS give myself a Christmas present. And on this particular year the present was a Carol party,—which is about as good fun, all things consenting kindly, as a man can have.

Many things must consent, as will appear. First of all there must be good sleighing,—and second, a fine night for Christmas eve. Ours are not the carollings of your poor shivering little East Angles or South Mercians, where they have to plod round afoot in countries where they do not know what a sleigh-ride is.

I had asked Harry to have sixteen of the best voices in the chapel school to be trained to eight or ten good Carols without knowing why. We did not care to disappoint them if a February thaw setting in on the 24th of December should break up the spree before it began. Then I had told Howland that he must reserve for me a span of good horses, and a sleigh that I could pack sixteen small children into, tight-stowed. Howland is always good about such things, knew what the sleigh was for, having done the same in other years, and doubled the span of horses of his own accord, because the children would like it better, and "it would be no difference to him." Sunday night as the weather nymphs ordered, the wind hauled round to the northwest and every-thing froze hard. Monday night, things moderated and the snow began to fall steadily,—so steadily;—and so Tuesday night the Metropolitan people gave up their unequal contest, all good men and angels rejoicing at their discomfiture, and only a few of the people in the very lowest *Bolgie*, being ill-natured enough to grieve. And thus it was, that by Thursday evening was one hard compact roadway from Copp's Hill to the Bone-burner's Gehenna, fit for good men and angels to ride over, without jar, without noise and without fatigue to horse or man. So it was that when I came down with Lycidas to the chapel at seven o'clock, I found Harry had gathered there his eight pretty girls and his eight jolly boys, and had them practising for the last time,

> "Carol, carol, Christians,
> Carol joyfully;
> Carol for the coming
> Of Christ's nativity."

I think the children had got inkling of what was coming, or perhaps

Harry had hinted it to their mothers. Certainly they were warmly dressed, and when, fifteen minutes afterwards, Howland came round himself with the sleigh, he had put in as many rugs and bear-skins as if he thought the children were to be taken new born from their respective cradles. Great was the rejoicing as the bells of the horses rang beneath the chapel windows, and Harry did not get his last *da capo* for his last carol. Not much matter indeed, for they were perfect enough in it before midnight.

Lycidas and I tumbled in on the back seat, each with a child in his lap to keep us warm; I was flanked by Sam Perry, and he by John Rich, both of the mercurial age, and therefore good to do errands. Harry was in front somewhere flanked in likewise, and the twelve other children lay in miscellaneously between, like sardines when you have first opened the box. I had invited Lycidas, because, besides being my best friend, he is the best fellow in the world, and so deserves the best Christmas eve can give him. Under the full moon, on the snow still white, with sixteen children at the happiest, and with the blessed memories of the best the world has ever had, there can be nothing better than two or three such hours.

"First, driver, out on Commonwealth Avenue. That will tone down the horses. Stop on the left after you have passed Fairfield Street." So we dashed up to the front of Haliburton's palace, where he was keeping his first Christmas tide. And the children, whom Harry had hushed down for a square or two, broke forth with good full voice under his strong lead in

"Shepherd of tender sheep,"

singing with all that unconscious pathos with which children do sing, and starting the tears in your eyes in the midst of your gladness. The instant the horses' bells stopped, their voices began. In an instant more we saw Haliburton and Anna run to the window and pull up the shades, and, in a minute more, faces at all the windows. And so the children sung through Clement's old hymn. Little did Clement think of bells and snow, as he taught it in his Sunday school there in Alexandria. But perhaps to-day, as they pin up the laurels and the palm in the chapel at Alexandria, they are humming the words, not thinking of Clement more than he thought of us. As the children closed with

"Swell the triumphant song
To Christ, our King,"

Haliburton came running out, and begged me to bring them in. But I told him, "No," as soon as I could hush their shouts of "Merry Christmas;" that we had a long journey before us, and must not alight by the way. And the children broke out with

> "Hail to the night,
> Hail to the day,"

rather a favorite,—quicker and more to the childish taste perhaps than the other,—and with another "Merry Christmas" we were off again.

Off, the length of Commonwealth Avenue, to where it crosses the Brookline branch of the Mill-Dam,—dashing along with the gayest of the sleighing-parties as we came back into town, up Chestnut Street, through Louisburg Square,—we ran the sleigh into a bank on the slope of Pinckney Street in front of Walter's house,—and, before they suspected there that any one had come, the children were singing

> "Carol, carol, Christians,
> Carol joyfully."

Kisses flung from the window; kisses flung back from the street. "Merry Christmas" again with a good-will, and then one of the girls began

> "When Anna took the baby,
> And pressed his lips to hers"—

and all of them fell in so cheerily. O dear me! it is a scrap of old Ephrem the Syrian, if they did but know it! And when, after this, Harry would fain have driven on, because two carols at one house was the rule, how the little witches begged that they might sing just one song more there, because Mrs. Alexander had been so kind to them, when she showed them about the German stitches. And then up the hill and over to the North End, and as far as we could get the horses up into Moon Court, that they might sing to the Italian image-man who gave Lucy the boy and dog in plaster, when she was sick in the spring. For the children had, you know, the choice of where they would go; and they select their best friends, and will be more apt to remember the Italian image-man than Chrysostom himself, though Chrysostom should have "made a few remarks" to them seventeen times in the chapel. Then the Italian image-man heard for the first time in his life

> "Now is the time of Christmas come,"

and

> "Jesus in his babes abiding."

And then we came up Hanover Street and stopped under Mr. Gerry's chapel, where they were dressing the walls with their evergreens, and gave them

"Hail to the night,
Hail to the day";

and so down State Street and stopped at the Advertiser office, because, when the boys gave their "Literary Entertainment," Mr. Hale put in their advertisement for nothing, and up in the old attic there the compositors were relieved to hear

"Nor war nor battle sound,"

and

"The waiting world was still."

Even the leading editor relaxed from his gravity, and the "In General" man from his more serious views, and the Daily the next morning wished everybody a merry Christmas with even more unction, and resolved that in coming years it would have a supplement, large enough to contain all the good wishes. So away again to the houses of confectioners who had given the children candy,—to Miss Simonds's house, because she had been so good to them in school,—to the palaces of millionnaires who had prayed for these children with tears if the children only knew it,—to Dr. Frothingham's in Summer Street, I remember, where we stopped because the Boston Association of Ministers met there,— and out on Dover Street Bridge, that the poor chair-mender might hear our carols sung once more before he heard them better sung in another world where nothing needs mending.

"King of glory, king of peace!"
"Hear the song, and see the Star!"
"Welcome be thou, heavenly King!"
"Was not Christ our Saviour?"

and all the others, rung out with order or without order, breaking the hush directly as the horses' bells were stilled, thrown into the air with all the gladness of childhood, selected sometimes as Harry happened to think best for the hearers, but more often as the jubilant and uncontrolled enthusiasm of the children bade them break out in the most joyous, least studied, and purely lyrical of all. O, we went to twenty places that night, I suppose! We went to the grandest places in Boston, and we went to the meanest. Everywhere they wished us a merry Christmas, and we them.

Everywhere a little crowd gathered round us, and then we dashed away far enough to gather quite another crowd; and then back, perhaps, not sorry to double on our steps if need were, and leaving every crowd with a happy thought of

"The star, the manger, and the Child!"

At nine we brought up at my house, D Street, three doors from the corner, and the children picked their very best for Polly and my six little girls to hear, and then for the first time we let them jump out and run in. Polly had some hot oysters for them, so that the frolic was crowned with a treat. There was a Christmas cake cut into sixteen pieces, which they took home to dream upon; and then hoods and muffs on again, and by ten o'clock, or a little after, we had all the girls and all the little ones at their homes. Four of the big boys, our two flankers and Harry's right and left hand men, begged that they might stay till the last moment. They could walk back from the stable, and "rather walk than not, indeed." To which we assented, having gained parental permission, as we left younger sisters in their respective homes.

CHAPTER II

Lycidas and I both thought, as we went into these modest houses, to leave the children, to say they had been good and to wish a "Merry Christmas" ourselves to fathers, mothers, and to guardian aunts, that the welcome of those homes was perhaps the best part of it all. Here was the great stout sailor-boy whom we had not seen since he came back from sea. He was a mere child when he left our school years on years ago, for the East, on board Perry's vessel, and had been round the world. Here was brave Mrs. Masury. I had not seen her since her mother died. "Indeed, Mr. Ingham, I got so used to watching then, that I cannot sleep well yet o' nights; I wish you knew some poor creature that wanted me to-night, if it were only in memory of Bethlehem." "You take a deal of trouble for the children," said Campbell, as he crushed my hand in his; "but you know they love you, and you know I would do as much for you and yours,"—which I knew was true. "What can I send to your children?" said Dalton, who was finishing sword-blades. (Ill wind was Fort Sumter, but it blew good to poor Dalton, whom it set up in the world with his sword-factory.) "Here's an old-fashioned tape-measure for the girl, and a Sheffield wimble for the boy. What, there is no boy? Let one of the girls have it then; it will count one more present for her." And so he pressed his brown-paper parcel into my hand. From every house, though it were the humblest, a word of love, as sweet, in truth, as if we could have heard the voice of angels singing in the sky.

I bade Harry good-night; took Lycidas to his lodgings, and gave his wife my Christmas wishes and good-night; and, coming down to the sleigh again, gave way to the feeling which I think you will all understand, that this was not the time to stop, but just the time to begin. For the streets were stiller now, and the moon brighter than ever, if possible, and the blessings of these simple people and of the grand people, and of the very angels in heaven, who are not bound to the misery of using words when they have anything worth saying,— all these wishes and blessings were round me, all the purity of the still winter night, and I didn't want to lose it all by going to bed to sleep. So I put the boys all together, where they could chatter, took one more brisk turn on the two avenues, and then, passing through Charles Street, I believe I was even thinking of Cambridge, I noticed the lights in Woodhull's house, and, seeing they were up, thought I would make Fanny a midnight call. She came to the door herself. I asked if she were waiting for Santa Claus, but saw in a moment that I must not joke with her. She said she had hoped I was her husband. In a minute was one of these contrasts which make life, life. God puts us into the world that we may try them and be tried by them. Poor Fanny's mother had been blocked up on the Springfield train as she was coming on to Christmas. The old lady had been chilled through, and was here in bed now with pneumonia. Both Fanny's children had been ailing when she came, and this morning the doctor had pronounced it scarlet fever. Fanny had not undressed herself since Monday, nor slept, I thought, in the same time. So while we had been singing carols and wishing merry Christmas, the poor child had been waiting, and hoping that her husband or Edward, both of whom were on the tramp, would find for her and bring to her the model nurse, who had not yet appeared. But at midnight this unknown sister had not arrived, nor had either of the men returned. When I rang, Fanny had hoped I was one of them. Professional paragons, dear reader, are shy of scarlet fever. I told the poor child that it was better as it was. I wrote a line for Sam Perry to take to his aunt, Mrs. Masury, in which I simply said: "Dear mamma, I have found the poor creature who wants you to-night. Come back in this carriage." I bade him take a hack at Barnard's, where they were all up waiting for the assembly to be done at Papanti's. I sent him over to Albany Street; and really as I sat there trying to soothe Fanny, it seemed to me less time than it has taken me to dictate this little story about her, before Mrs. Masury rang gently, and I left them, having made Fanny promise that she would consecrate the day, which at that moment was born, by trusting God, by going to bed and going to sleep, knowing that her children were in much better hands than hers. As I passed out of the hall, the gas-light fell on a print of Correggio's Adoration, where Woodhull had himself written years before,

"Ut appareat iis qui in tenebris et umbra mortis positi sunt."

"Darkness and the shadow of death" indeed, and what light like the light and comfort such a woman as my Mary Masury brings!

And so, but for one of the accidents, as we call them, I should have dropped the boys at the corner of Dover Street, and gone home with my Christmas lesson.

But it happened, as we irreverently say,—it happened as we crossed Park Square, so called from its being an irregular pentagon of which one of the sides has been taken away, that I recognized a tall man, plodding across in the snow, head down, round-shouldered, stooping forward in walking, with his right shoulder higher than his left; and by these tokens I knew Tom Coram, prince among Boston princes. Not Thomas Coram that built the Foundling Hospital, though he was of Boston too; but he was longer ago. You must look for him in Addison's contribution to a supplement to the Spectator,—the old Spectator, I mean, not the Thursday Spectator, which is more recent. Not Thomas Coram, I say, but Tom Coram, who would build a hospital to-morrow, if you showed him the need, without waiting to die first, and always helps forward, as a prince should, whatever is princely, be it a statue at home, a school at Richmond, a newspaper in Florida, a church in Exeter, a steam-line to Liverpool, or a widow who wants a hundred dollars. I wished him a merry Christmas, and Mr. Howland, by a fine instinct, drew up the horses as I spoke. Coram shook hands; and, as it seldom happens that I have an empty carriage while he is on foot, I asked him if I might not see him home. He was glad to get in. We wrapped him up with spoils of the bear, the fox, and the bison, turned the horses' heads again,—five hours now since they started on this entangled errand of theirs,—and gave him his ride. "I was thinking of you at the moment," said Coram,— "thinking of old college times, of the mystery of language as unfolded by the Abbé Faria to Edmond Dantes in the depths of the Chateau d'If. I was wondering if you could teach me Japanese, if I asked you to a Christmas dinner." I laughed. Japan was really a novelty then, and I asked him since when he had been in correspondence with the sealed country. It seemed that their house at Shanghae had just sent across there their agents for establishing the first house in Edomo, in Japan, under the new treaty. Everything looked promising, and the beginnings were made for the branch which has since become Dot and Trevilyan there. Of this he had the first tidings in his letters by the mail of that afternoon. John Coram, his brother, had written to him, and had said that he enclosed for his amusement the Japanese bill of particulars, as it had been drawn out, on which they had founded their orders for the first assorted cargo ever to be sent from America to Edomo. Bill of particulars there was, stretching down the long tissue-paper in exquisite chirography. But by some freak of the "total depravity of things," the translated order for the assorted cargo was not there. John Coram, in his care to fold up the Japanese writing nicely, had left on his own desk at Shanghae the more intelligible English. "And so I must wait," said Tom philosophically, "till the next East India mail for my orders, certain that seven English houses have had less enthusiastic and philological correspondents than my brother."

I said I did not see that. That I could not teach him to speak the Taghalian dialects so well, that he could read them with facility before Saturday. But I could do a good deal better. Did he remember writing a note to old Jack Percival for me five years ago? No, he remembered no such thing; he knew Jack Percival, but never wrote a note to him in his life. Did he remember giving me fifty dollars, because I had taken a delicate boy, whom I was going to send to sea, and I was not quite satisfied with the government outfit? No, he did not remember that, which was not strange, for that was a thing he was doing every day. "Well, I don't care how much you remember, but the boy about whom you wrote to Jack Percival, for whose mother's ease of mind you provided the half-hundred, is back again,—strong, straight, and well; what is more to the point, he had the whole charge of Perry's commissariat on shore at Yokohama, was honorably discharged out there, reads Japanese better than you read English; and if it will help you at all, he shall be here at your house at breakfast." For as I spoke we stopped at Coram's door. "Ingham," said Coram, "if you were not a parson, I should say you were romancing." "My child," said I, "I sometimes write a parable for the Atlantic; but the words of my lips are verity, as all those of the Sandemanians. Go to bed; do not even dream of the Taghalian dialects; be sure that the Japanese interpreter will breakfast with you, and the next time you are in a scrape send for the nearest minister. George, tell your brother Ezra that Mr. Coram wishes him to breakfast here to-morrow morning at eight o'clock; don't forget the number, Pemberton Square, you know." "Yes, sir," said George; and Thomas Coram laughed, said "Merry Christmas," and we parted.

It was time we were all in bed, especially these boys. But glad enough am I as I write these words that the meeting of Coram set us back that dropped-stitch in our night's journey. There was one more delay. We were sweeping by the Old State House, the boys singing again, "Carol, carol, Christians," as we dashed along the still streets, when I caught sight of Adams Todd, and he recognized me. He had heard us singing when we were at the Advertiser office. Todd is an old fellow-apprentice of mine,—and he is now, or rather was that night, chief pressman in the Argus office. I like the Argus people,—it was there that I was South American Editor, now many years ago,—and they befriend me to this hour. Todd hailed me, and once more I stopped. "What sent you out from your warm steam-boiler?" "Steam-boiler, indeed," said Todd. "Two rivets loose,—steam-room full of steam,—police frightened,—neighborhood in a row,—and we had to put out the fire. She would have run a week without hurting a fly,—only a little puff in the street sometimes. But there we are, Ingham. We shall lose the early mail as it stands. Seventy-eight tokens to be worked now." They always talked largely of their edition at the Argus. Saw it with many eyes, perhaps; but this time, I am sure, Todd spoke true. I caught his idea at once. In younger and more muscular times, Todd and I had worked the Adams press by that fly-wheel for full five minutes at a time, as a test of strength; and in my mind's eye, I saw that he was printing his paper at this moment with relays of grinding stevedores. He said it was so. "But think of it to-night," said he. "It is Christmas eve, and not an Irishman to be hired, though one paid him ingots. Not a man can stand the grind ten minutes." I knew that very well from old experience, and I thanked him inwardly for not saying "the demnition grind," with Mantilini. "We cannot run the press half the time," said he; "and the men we have are giving out now. We shall lose all our carrier delivery." "Todd," said I, "is this a night to be talking of ingots, or hiring, or losing, or gaining? When will you learn that Love rules the court, the camp, and the Argus office." And I wrote on the back of a letter to Campbell: "Come to the Argus office, No. 2 Dassett's Alley, with seven men not afraid to work"; and I gave it to John and Sam, bade Howland take the boys to Campbell's house,—walked down with Todd to his office,—challenged him to take five minutes at the wheel, in memory of old times,—made the tired relays laugh as they saw us take hold; and then,—when I had cooled off, and put on my Cardigan,—met Campbell, with his seven sons of Anak, tumbling down the stairs, wondering what round of mercy the parson had found for them this time. I started home, knowing I should now have my Argus with my coffee.

CHAPTER III

*A*nd so I walked home. Better so, perhaps, after all, than in the lively sleigh, with the tinkling bells.

"It was a calm and silent night!—
    Seven hundred years and fifty-three
Had Rome been growing up to might,
    And now was queen of land and sea!

No sound was heard of clashing wars,—
    Peace brooded o'er the hushed domain;
Apollo, Pallas, Jove, and Mars
    Held undisturbed their ancient reign
        In the solemn midnight,
            Centuries ago!"

What an eternity it seemed since I started with those children singing carols. Bethlehem, Nazareth, Calvary, Rome, Roman senators, Tiberius, Paul, Nero, Clement, Ephrem, Ambrose, and all the singers,—Vincent de Paul, and all the loving wonder-workers, Milton and Herbert and all the carol-writers, Luther and Knox and all the prophets,—what a world of people had been keeping Christmas with Sam Perry and Lycidas and Harry and me; and here were Yokohama and the Japanese, the Daily Argus and its ten million tokens and their readers,—poor Fanny Woodhull and her sick mother there, keeping Christmas too! For a finite world, these are a good many "waits" to be singing in one poor fellow's ears on one Christmas tide.

" 'Twas in the calm and silent night!—
    The senator of haughty Rome,
Impatient urged his chariot's flight,
    From lordly revel, rolling home.
Triumphal arches gleaming swell
    His breast, with thoughts of boundless sway.
What recked the *Roman* what befell
    A paltry province far away,
        In the solemn midnight,
            Centuries ago!

"Within that province far away
 Went plodding home a weary boor;
A streak of light before him lay,
 Fallen through a half-shut stable door
Across his path. He passed,—for naught
 Told *what was going on within*;
How keen the stars, his only thought,
 The air how calm and cold and thin,
  In the solemn midnight,
   Centuries ago!"

"Streak of light"—Is there a light in Lycidas's room? They not in bed! That is making a night of it! Well, there are few hours of the day or night when I have not been in Lycidas's room, so I let myself in by the night-key he gave me, ran up the stairs,—it is a horrid seven-storied, first-class lodging-house. For my part, I had as lief live in a steeple. Two flights I ran up, two steps at a time,—I was younger then than I am now,—pushed open the door which was ajar, and saw such a scene of confusion as I never saw in Mary's over-nice parlor before. Queer! I remember the first thing that I saw was wrong was a great ball of white German worsted on the floor. Her basket was upset. A great Christmas-tree lay across the rug, quite too high for the room; a large sharp-pointed Spanish clasp-knife was by it, with which they had been lopping it; there were two immense baskets of white papered presents, both upset; but what frightened me most was the centre-table. Three or four handkerchiefs on it,—towels, napkins, I know not what,—all brown and red and almost black with blood! I turned, heart-sick, to look into the bedroom,—and I really had a sense of relief when I saw somebody. Bad enough it was, however. Lycidas, but just now so strong and well, lay pale and exhausted on the bloody bed, with the clothing removed from his right thigh and leg, while over him bent Mary and Morton. I learned afterwards that poor Lycidas, while trimming the Christmas-tree, and talking merrily with Mary and Morton,—who, by good luck, had brought round his presents late, and was staying to tie on glass balls and apples,—had given himself a deep and dangerous wound with the point of the unlucky knife, and had lost a great deal of blood before the hemorrhage could be controlled. Just before I entered, the stick tourniquet which Morton had improvised had slipped in poor Mary's unpractised hand, at the moment he was about to secure the bleeding artery, and the blood followed in such a gush as compelled him to give his whole attention to stopping its flow. He only knew my entrance by the "Ah, Mr. Ingham," of the frightened Irish girl, who stood useless behind the head of the bed.

"O Fred," said Morton, without looking up, "I am glad you are here."

"And what can I do for you?"

"Some whiskey,—first of all."

"There are two bottles," said Mary, who was holding the candle,—"in the cupboard, behind his dressing-glass."

I took Bridget with me, struck a light in the dressing-room (how she blundered about the match), and found the cupboard door locked! Key doubtless in Mary's pocket,—probably in pocket of "another dress." I did not ask. Took my own bunch, willed tremendously that my account-book drawer key should govern the lock, and it did. If it had not, I should have put my fist through the panels. Bottle of bedbug poison; bottle marked "bay rum"; another bottle with no mark; two bottles of Saratoga water. "Set them all on the floor, Bridget." A tall bottle of Cologne. Bottle marked in MS. What in the world is it? "Bring that candle, Bridget." "Eau destillée. Marron, Montreal." What in the world did Lycidas bring distilled water from Montreal for? And then Morton's clear voice in the other room, "As quick as you can, Fred." "Yes! in one moment. Put all these on the floor, Bridget." Here they are at last. "Bourbon whiskey." "Corkscrew, Bridget."

"Indade, sir, and where is it?" "Where? I don't know. Run down as quick as you can, and bring it. His wife cannot leave him." So Bridget ran, and the first I heard was the rattle as she pitched down the last six stairs of the first flight headlong. Let us hope she has not broken her leg. I meanwhile am driving a silver pronged fork into the Bourbon corks, and the blade of my own penknife on the other side.

"Now, Fred," from George within. (We all call Morton "George.") "Yes, in one moment," I replied. Penknife blade breaks off, fork pulls right out, two crumbs of cork come with it. Will that girl never come?

I turned round; I found a goblet on the washstand; I took Lycidas's heavy clothes-brush, and knocked off the neck of the bottle. Did you ever do it, reader, with one of those pressed glass bottles they make now? It smashed like a Prince Rupert's drop in my hand, crumbled into seventy pieces,—a nasty smell of whiskey on the floor,—and I, holding just the hard bottom of the thing with two large spikes running worthless up into the air. But I seized the goblet, poured into it what was left in the bottom, and carried it in to Morton as quietly as I could. He bade me give Lycidas as much as he could swallow; then showed me how to substitute my thumb for his, and compress the great artery. When he was satisfied that he could trust me, he began his work again, silently; just speaking what must be said to that brave Mary, who seemed to have three hands because he needed them. When all was secure, he glanced at the ghastly white face, with beads of perspiration on the forehead and upper lip, laid his finger on the pulse, and said: "We will have a little more whiskey. No, Mary, you are overdone already; let Fred bring it." The truth was that poor Mary was almost as white as Lycidas. She would not faint,—that was the only reason she did not,—and at the moment I wondered that she did not fall. I believe George and I were both expecting it, now the excitement was over. He called her Mary, and me Fred, because we were all together every day of our lives. Bridget, you see, was still nowhere.

So I retired for my whiskey again,—to attack that other bottle. George whispered quickly as I went, "Bring enough,—bring the bottle." Did he want the bottle corked? Would that Kelt ever come up stairs? I passed the bell-rope as I went into the dressing-room, and rang as hard as I could ring. I took the other bottle, and bit steadily with my teeth at the cork, only, of course, to wrench the end of it off. George called me, and I stepped back. "No," said he, "bring your whiskey."

Mary had just rolled gently back on the floor. I went again in despair. But I heard Bridget's step this time. First flight, first passage; second flight, second passage. She ran in in triumph at length, with a *screw-driver*!

"No!" I whispered,—"no. The crooked thing you draw corks with," and I showed her the bottle again. "Find one somewhere and don't come back without it." So she vanished for the second time.

"Frederic!" said Morton. I think he never called me so before. Should I risk the clothes-brush again? I opened Lycidas's own drawers,—papers, boxes, everything in order,—not a sign of a tool.

"Frederic!" "Yes," I said. But why did I say "Yes"? "Father of Mercy, tell me what to do."

And my mazed eyes, dim with tears,—did you ever shed tears from excitement?—fell on an old razor-strop of those days of shaving, made by C. Whittaker, SHEFFIELD. The "Sheffield" stood in black letters out from the rest like a vision. They make corkscrews in Sheffield too. If this Whittaker had only made a corkscrew! And what is a "Sheffield wimble"?

Hand in my pocket,—brown paper parcel.

"Where are you, Frederic?" "Yes," said I, for the last time. Twine off! brown paper off. And I learned that the "Sheffield wimble" was one of those things whose name you never heard before, which people sell you in Thames Tunnel, where a hoof-cleaner, a gimlet, a screw-driver, and a *corkscrew* fold into one handle.

"Yes," said I, again. "Pop," said the cork. "Bubble, bubble, bubble," said the whiskey. Bottle in one hand, full tumbler in the other, I walked in. George poured half a tumblerful down Lycidas's throat that time. Nor do I dare say how much he poured down afterwards. I found that there was need of it, from what he said of the pulse, when it was all over. I guess Mary had some, too.

This was the turning-point. He was exceedingly weak, and we sat by him in turn through the night, giving, at short intervals, stimulants and such food as he could swallow easily; for I remember Morton was very particular not to raise his head more than we could help. But there was no real danger after this.

As we turned away from the house on Christmas morning,—I to preach and he to visit his patients,—he said to me, "Did you make that whiskey?"

"No," said I, "but poor Dod Dalton had to furnish the corkscrew."

And I went down to the chapel to preach. The sermon had been lying ready at home on my desk,—and Polly had brought it round to me,—for there had been no time for me to go from Lycidas's home to D Street and to return. There was the text, all as it was the day before:—

> "They helped every one his neighbor, and every one said to his brother, Be of good courage. So the carpenter encouraged the goldsmith, and he that smootheth with the hammer him that smote the anvil."

And there were the pat illustrations, as I had finished them yesterday; of the comfort Mary Magdalen gave Joanna, the court lady; and the comfort the court lady gave Mary Magdalen, after the mediator of a new covenant had mediated between them; how Simon the Cyrenian, and Joseph of Arimathea, and the beggar Bartimeus comforted each other, gave each other strength, common force, *com-fort*, when the One Life flowed in all their veins; how on board the ship the Tent-Maker proved to be Captain, and the Centurion learned his duty from his Prisoner, and how they "*All* came safe to shore," because the New Life was there. But as I preached, I caught Frye's eye. Frye is always critical; and I said to myself, "Frye would not take his illustrations from eighteen hundred years ago." And I saw dear old Dod Dalton trying to keep awake, and Campbell hard asleep after trying, and Jane Masury looking round to see if her mother did not come in; and Ezra Sheppard, looking, not so much at me, as at the window beside me, as if his thoughts were the other side of the world. And I said to them all, "O, if I could tell you, my friends, what every twelve hours of my life tells me,—of the way in which woman helps woman, and man helps man, when only the ice is broken,—how we are all rich so soon as we find out that we are all brothers, and how we are all in want, unless we can call at any moment for a brother's hand,—then I could make you understand something, in the lives you lead every day, of what the New Covenant, the New Commonwealth, the New Kingdom is to be."

But I did not dare tell Dod Dalton what Campbell had been doing for Todd, nor did I dare tell Campbell by what unconscious arts old Dod had been help-ing Lycidas. Perhaps the sermon would have been better had I done so.

But, when we had our tree in the evening at home, I did tell all this story to Polly and the bairns, and I gave Alice her measuring-tape,—precious with a spot of Lycidas's blood,—and Bertha her Sheffield wimble. "Papa," said old Clara, who is the next child, "all the people gave presents, did not they, as they did in the picture in your study?"

"Yes," said I, "though they did not all know they were giving them."

"Why do they not give such presents every day?" said Clara.

"O child," I said, "it is only for thirty-six hours of the three hundred and sixty-five days, that all people remember that they are all brothers and sisters, and those are the hours that we call, therefore, Christmas eve and Christmas day."

"And when they always remember it," said Bertha, "it will be Christmas all the time! What fun!"

"What fun, to be sure; but, Clara, what is in the picture?"

"Why, an old woman has brought eggs to the baby in the manger, and an old man has brought a sheep. I suppose they all brought what they had."

"I suppose those who came from Sharon brought roses," said Bertha. And Alice, who is eleven, and goes to the Lincoln School, and there-fore knows every thing, said,—"Yes, and the Damascus people brought Damascus wimbles."

"This is certain," said Polly, "that nobody tried to give a straw, but the straw, if he really gave it, carried a blessing."

Alice's Christmas-Tree

CHAPTER I

Alice Macneil had made the plan of this Christmas-tree, all by herself and for herself. She had a due estimate of those manufactured trees which hard-worked "Sabbath Schools" get up for rewards of merit for the children who have been regular, and at the last moment have saved attendance-tickets enough. Nor did Alice MacNeil sit in judgment on these. She had a due estimate of them. But for her Christmas-tree she had two plans not included in those more meritorious buddings and bourgeonings of the winter. First, she meant to get it up without any help from anybody. And, secondly, she meant that the boys and girls who had anything from it should be regular laners and by-way farers,—they were to have no tickets of respectability,—they were not in any way to buy their way in; but, for this once, those were to come in to a Christmas-tree who happened to be ragged and in the streets when the Christmas-tree was ready.

So Alice asked Mr. Williams, the minister, if she could have one of the rooms in the vestry when Christmas eve came; and he, good saint, was only too glad to let her. He offered, gently, his assistance in sifting out the dirty boys and girls, intimating to Alice that there was dirt and dirt; and that, even in those lowest depths which she was plunging into, there were yet lower deeps which she might find it wise to shun. But here Alice told him frankly that she would rather try her experiment fairly through. Perhaps she was wrong, but she would like to see that she was wrong in her own way. Any way, on Christmas eve, she wanted no distinctions.

That part of her plan went bravely forward.

Her main difficulty came on the other side,—that she had too many to help her. She was not able to carry out the first part of her plan, and make or buy all her presents herself. For everybody was pleased with this notion of a truly catholic or universal tree; and everybody wanted to help. Well, if anybody would send her a box of dominos, or a jack-knife, or an open-eye-shut-eye doll, who was Alice to say it should not go on the tree? and when Mrs. Hesperides sent round a box of Fayal oranges, who was Alice to say that the children should not have oranges? And when Mr. Gorham Parsons sent in well-nigh a barrel full of Hubbardston None-such apples, who was Alice to say they should not have apples? So the tree grew and grew, and bore more and more fruit, till it was clear that there would be more than eighty reliable presents on it, besides apples and oranges, almonds and raisins galore.

Now you see this was a very great enlargement of Alice's plan; and it brought her to grief, as you shall see. She had proposed a cosey little tree for fifteen or twenty children. Well, if she had held to that, she would have had no more than she and Lillie, and Mr. Williams, and Mr. Gilmore, and John Flagg, and I, could have managed easily, particularly if mamma was there too. There would have been room enough in the chapel parlor; and it would have been, as I believe, just the pretty and cheerful Christmas jollity that Alice meant it should be. But when it came to eighty presents, and a company of eighty of the unwashed and unticketed, it became quite a different thing.

For now Alice began to fear that there would not be children enough in the highways and by-ways. So she started herself, as evening drew on, with George, the old faithful black major-domo, and she walked through the worst streets she knew anything of, of all those near the chapel; and, whenever she saw a brat particularly dirty, or a group of brats particularly forlorn, she sailed up gallantly, and, though she was frightened to death, she invited them to the tree. She gave little admittance cards, that said, "7 o'clock, Christmas Eve, 507 Livingstone Avenue," for fear the children would not remember. And she told Mr. Flagg that he and Mr. Gilmore might take some cards and walk out toward Williamsburg, and do the same thing, only they were to be sure that they asked the dirtiest and most forlorn children they saw. There was a friendly policeman with whom Alice had been brought into communication by the boys in her father's office, and he also was permitted to give notice of the tree. But he was also to be at the street door, armed with the strong arm of "The People of New York," and when the full quota of eighty had been admitted he was to admit no more.

Ah me! My poor Alice issued her cards only too freely. Better indeed, it seemed, had she held to her original plan; at least she thought so, and thinks so to this day. But I am not so certain. A hard time she had of it, however. Quarter of seven found the little Arabs in crowds around the door, with hundreds of others who thought they also were to find out what a "free lunch" was. The faithful officer Purdy was in attendance also; he passed in all who had the cards; he sent away legions, let me say, who had reason to dread him; but still there assembled a larger and larger throng about the door. Alice and Lillie, and the young gentlemen, and Mrs. MacNeil, were all at work up stairs, and the tree was a perfect beauty at last. They lighted up, and nothing could have been more lovely.

"Let them in!" said John Flagg rushing to the door, where expectant knocks had been heard already. "Let them in,—the smallest girls first!"

"Smallest girls," indeed! The door swung open, and a tide of boy and girl, girl and boy, boy big to hobble-de-hoy-dom, and girl big to young-woman-dom, came surging in, wildly screaming, scolding, pushing, and pulling. Omitting the profanity, these are the Christmas carols that fell on Alice's ear.

"Out o' that!" "Take that, then!" "Who are you?" "Hold your jaw!" "Can't you behave decent?" "You lie!" "Get out of my light!" "Oh, dear! you killed me!" "Who's killed?" "Golly! see there!" "I say, ma'am, give me that pair of skates!" "Shut up—" and so on, the howls being more and more impertinent, as the shepherds who had come to adore became more and more used to the position they were in.

Young Gilmore, who was willing to oblige Alice, but was not going to stand any nonsense, and would have willingly knocked the heads together of any five couples of this rebel rout, mounted on a corner of the railing, which, by Mr. Williams's prescience had been built around the tree, and addressed the riotous assembly.

They stopped to hear him, supposing he was to deliver the gifts, to which they had been summoned.

He told them pretty roundly that if they did not keep the peace, and stop crowding and yelling, they should all be turned out of doors; that they were to pass the little girls and boys forward first, and that nobody would have any thing to eat till this was done.

Some approach to obedience followed. A few little waifs were found, who in decency could be called *little* girls and boys. But, alas! as she looked down from her chair, Alice felt as if most of her guests looked like shameless, hulking big boys and big girls, only too well fitted to grapple with the world, and only too eager to accept its gifts without grappling. She and Lillie tried to forget this. They kissed a few little girls, and saw the faintest gleam of pleasure on one or two little faces. But there, also, the pleasure was almost extinct, in fear of the big boys and big girls howling around.

So the howling began again, as the distribution went forward. "Give me that jack-knife!" "I say, Mister, I'm as big as he is," "He had one before and hid it," "Be down, Tom Mulligan,—get off that fence or I'll hide you," "I don't want the book, give me them skates," "You sha'n't have the skates, I'll have 'em myself—" and so on. John Flagg finally knocked down Tom Mulligan, who had squeezed round behind the tree, in an effort to steal something, and had the satisfaction of sending him bellowing from the room, with his face covered with blood from his nose. Gilmore, meanwhile, was rapidly distributing an orange and an apple to each, which, while the oranges were sucked, gave a moment's quiet. Alice and the ladies, badly frightened, were stripping the tree as fast as they could, and at last announced that it was all clear, with almost as eager joy as half an hour before they had announced that it was all full. "There's a candy horn on top, give me that." "Give me that little apple." "Give me the old sheep." "Hoo! hurrah, for the old sheep!" This of a little lamb which had been placed as an appropriate ornament in front. Then began a howl about oranges. "I want another orange." "Bill's got some, and I've got none." "I say, Mister, give me an orange."

To which Mister replied, by opening the window, and speaking into the street,—"I say, Purdy, call four officers and come up and clear this room."

The room did not wait for the officers: it cleared itself very soon on this order, and was left a scene of wreck and dirt. Orange-peel trampled down on the floor; cake thrown down and mashed to mud, intermixed with that which had come in on boots, and the water which had been slobbered over from hasty mugs; the sugar plums which had fallen in scrambles, and little sprays of green too, trodden into the mass,—all made an aspect of filth like a market side-walk. And poor Alice was half crying and half laughing; poor Lillie was wholly crying. Gilmore and Flagg were explaining to each other how gladly they would have thrashed the whole set.

The thought uppermost in Alice's mind was that she had been a clear, out and out fool! And that, probably, is the impression of the greater part of the readers of her story,—or would have been the impression of any one who only had her point of view.

CHAPTER II

Perhaps the reader is willing to take another point of view.

As the group stood there, talking over the riot as Mrs. MacNeil called it,—as John Flagg tried to make Alice laugh by bringing her a half-piece of frosted pound-cake, and proving to her that it had not been on the floor,—as she said, her eyes streaming with tears, "I tell you, John! I am a fool, and I know I am, and nobody but a fool would have started such a row,"—as all this happened, Patrick Crehore came back for his little sister's orange which he had wrapped in her handkerchief and left on one of the book-racks in the room. Patrick was alone now, and was therefore sheepish enough, and got himself and his orange out of the room as soon as he well could. But he was sharp enough to note the whole position, and keen enough to catch Alice's words as she spoke to Mr. Flagg. Indeed, the general look of disappointment and chagrin in the room, and the contrast between this filthy ruin and the pretty elegance of half an hour ago, were distinct enough to be observed by a much more stupid boy than Patrick Crehore. He went down stairs and found Bridget waiting, and walked home with the little toddler, meditating rather more than was his wont on Alice's phrase, "I tell you, I am a fool." Meditating on it, he hauled Bridget up five flights of stairs and broke in on the little room where a table spread with a plentiful supply of tea, baker's bread, butter, cheese, and cabbage, waited their return. Jerry Crehore, his father, sat smoking, and his mother was tidying up the room.

"And had ye a good time, me darling? And ye 've brought home your orange, and a doll too, and mittens too. And what did you have, Pat?"

So Pat explained, almost sulkily, that he had a checker-board, and a set of checker-men, which he produced; but he put them by as if he hated the sight of them, and for a minute dropped the subject, while he helped little Biddy to cabbage. He ate something himself, drank some tea, and then delivered his rage with much unction, a little profanity, great incoherency,— but to his own relief.

"It's a mean thing it is, all of it," said he, "I'll be hanged but it is! I dunno who the lady is; but we've made her cry bad, I know that; and the boys acted like Nick. They knew that as well as I do. The man there had to knock one of the fellows down, bedad, and served him right, too. I say, the fellows fought, and hollared, and stole, and sure ye 'd thought ye was driving pigs down the Eighth Avenue, and I was as bad as the worst of 'em. That's what the boys did when a lady asked 'em to Christmas."

"That was a mean thing to do," said Jerry, taking his pipe from his mouth for a longer speech than he had ever been known to make while smoking.

Mrs. Crehore stopped in her dish-wiping, sat down, and gave her opinion. She did not know what a Christmas-tree was, having never seed one nor heared of one. But she did know that those who went to see a lady should show manners and behave like jintlemen, or not go at all. She expressed her conviction that Tom Mulligan was rightly served, and her regret that he had not two black eyes instead of one. She would have been glad, indeed, if certain Floyds, and Sullivans, and Flahertys with whose names of baptism she was better acquainted than I am, had shared a similar fate.

This oration, and the oracle of his father still more, appeased Pat somewhat; and when his supper was finished, after long silence, he said, "We'll give her a Christmas present. We will. Tom Mulligan and Bill Floyd and I will give it. The others sha'n't know. I know what we'll give her. I'll tell Bill Floyd that we made her cry."

CHAPTER III

After supper, accordingly, Pat Crehore repaired to certain rendezvous of the younger life of the neighborhood, known to him, in search of Bill Floyd. Bill was not at the first, nor at the second, there being indeed no rule or principle known to men or even to archangels by which Bill's presence at any particular spot at any particular time could be definitely stated. But Bill also, in his proud free-will, obeyed certain general laws; and accordingly Pat found him inspecting, as a volunteer officer of police, the hauling out and oiling of certain hose at the house of a neighboring hose company. "Come here, Bill. I got something to show you."

Bill had already carried home and put in safe keeping a copy of Routledge's "Robinson Crusoe," which had been given to him.

He left the hose inspection willingly, and hurried along with Pat, past many attractive groups, not even stopping where a brewer's horse had fallen on the ground, till Pat brought him in triumph to the gaudy window of a shoe-shop, lighted up gayly and full of the wares by which even shoe-shops lure in customers for Christmas.

"See there!" said Pat, nearly breathless. And he pointed to the very centre of the display, a pair of slippers made from bronze-gilt kid, and displaying a hideous blue silk bow upon the gilding. For what class of dancers or of maskers these slippers may have been made, or by what canon of beauty, I know not. Only they were the centre of decoration in the shoe-shop window. Pat looked at them with admiration, as he had often done, and said again to Bill Floyd, "See there, ain't them handsome?"

"Golly!" said Bill, "I guess so."

"Bill, let's buy them little shoes, and give 'em to her."

"Give 'em to who?" said Bill, from whose mind the Christmas-tree had for the moment faded, under the rivalry of the hose company, the brewer's horse, and the shop window. "Give 'em to who?"

"Why, her, I don't know who she is. The gal that made the what-do-ye-call-it, the tree, you know, and give us the oranges, where old Purdy was. I say, Bill, it was a mean dirty shame to make such a row there, when we was bid to a party; and I want to make the gal a present, for I see her crying, Bill. Crying cos it was such a row." Again, I omit certain profane expressions which did not add any real energy to the declaration.

"They is handsome," said Bill, meditatingly. "Ain't the blue ones handsomest?"

"No," said Pat, who saw he had gained his lodgment, and that the carrying his point was now only a matter of time. "The gould ones is the ones for me. We'll give 'em to the gal for a Christmas present, you and I and Tom Mulligan."

Bill Floyd did not dissent, being indeed in the habit of going as he was led, as were most of the "rebel rout" with whom he had an hour ago been acting. He assented entirely to Pat's proposal. By "Christmas" both parties understood that the present was to be made before Twelfth Night, not necessarily on Christmas day. Neither of them had a penny; but both of them knew, perfectly well, that whenever they chose to get a little money they could do so.

They soon solved their first question, as to the cost of the coveted slippers. True, they knew, of course, that they would be ejected from the decent shop if they went in to inquire. But, by lying in wait, they soon discovered Delia Sullivan, a decent-looking girl they knew, passing by, and having made her their confidant, so far that she was sure she was not fooled, they sent her in to inquire. The girl returned to announce, to the astonishment of all parties, that the shoes cost six dollars.

"Hew!" cried Pat, "six dollars for them are! I bought my mother's new over-shoes for one." But not the least did he 'bate of his determination, and he and Bill Floyd went in search of Tom Mulligan.

Tom was found as easily as Bill. But it was not so easy to enlist him. Tom was in a regular corner liquor store with men who were sitting smoking, drinking, and telling dirty stories. Either of the other boys would have been whipped at home if he had been known to be seen sitting in this place, and the punishment would have been well bestowed. But Tom Mulligan had had nobody thrash him for many a day till John Flagg had struck out so smartly from the shoulder. Perhaps, had there been some thrashing as discriminating as Jerry Flaherty's, it had been better for Tom Mulligan. The boys found him easily enough, but, as I said, had some difficulty in getting him away. With many assurances, however, that they had something to tell him, and something to show him, they lured him from the shadow of the comfortable stove into the night.

Pat Crehore, who had more of the tact of oratory than he knew, then boldly told Tom Mulligan the story of the Christmas-tree, as it passed after Tom's ejection. Tom was sour at first, but soon warmed to the narrative, and even showed indignation at the behavior of boys who had seemed to carry themselves less obnoxiously than he did. All the boys agreed, that but for certain others who had never been asked to come, and ought to be ashamed to be there with them as were, there would have been no row. They all agreed that on some suitable occasion unknown to me and to this story they would take vengeance on these Tidds and Sullivans. When Pat Crehore wound up his statement, by telling how he saw the ladies crying, and all the pretty room looking like a pig-sty, Tom Mulligan was as loud as he was in saying that it was all wrong, and that nobody but blackguards would have joined in it, in particular such blackguards as the Tidds and Sullivans above alluded to.

Then to Tom's sympathizing ear was confided the project of the gold shoes, as the slippers were always called, in this honorable company. And Tom completely approved. He even approved the price. He explained to the others that it would be mean to give to a lady any thing of less price. This was exactly the sum which recommended itself to his better judgment. And so the boys went home, agreeing to meet Christmas morning as a Committee of Ways and Means.

To the discussions of this committee I need not admit you. Many plans were proposed: one that they should serve through the holidays at certain ten-pin alleys, known to them; one that they should buy off Fogarty from his newspaper route for a few days. But the decision was, that Pat, the most decent in appearance, should dress up in a certain Sunday suit he had, and offer the services of himself, and two unknown friends of his, as extra cork-boys at Birnebaum's brewery, where Tom Mulligan reported they were working nights, that they might fill an extra order. This device succeeded. Pat and his friends were put on duty, for trial, on the night of the 26th; and, the foreman of the corking-room being satisfied, they retained their engagements till New Year's eve, when they were paid three dollars each, and resigned their positions.

"Let's buy her three shoes!" said Bill, in enthusiasm at their success. But this proposal was rejected. Each of the other boys had a private plan for an extra present to "her" by this time. The sacred six dollars was folded up in a bit of straw paper from the brewery, and the young gentlemen went home to make their toilets, a process they had had no chance to go through, on Christmas eve. After this, there was really no difficulty about their going into the shoe-shop, and none about consummating the purchase,—to the utter astonishment of the dealer. The gold shoes were bought, rolled up in paper, and ready for delivery.

Bill Floyd had meanwhile learned, by inquiry at the chapel, where she lived, though there were doubts whether any of them knew her name. The others rejected his proposals that they should take street cars, and they boldly pushed afoot up to Clinton Avenue, and rang, not without terror, at the door.

Terror did not diminish when black George appeared, whose acquaintance they had made at the tree. But fortunately George did not recognize them in their apparel of elegance. When they asked for the "lady that gave the tree," he bade them wait a minute, and in less than a minute Alice came running out to meet them. To the boys' great delight, she was not crying now.

"If you please, ma'am," said Tom, who had been commissioned as spokesman,—"if you please, them 's our Christmas present to you, ma'am. Them 's gold shoes. And please, ma'am, we're very sorry there was such a row at the Christmas, ma'am. It was mean, ma'am. Good-by, ma'am."

Alice's eyes were opening wider and wider, nor at this moment did she understand. "Gold shoes," and "row at the Christmas," stuck by her, however; and she understood there was a present. So, of course, she said the right thing, by accident, and did the right thing, being a lady through and through.

"No, you must not go away. Come in, boys, come in. I did not know you, you know." As how should she. "Come in and sit down."

"Can't ye take off your hat?" said Tom, in an aside to Pat, who had neglected this reverence as he entered. And Tom was thus a little established in his own esteem.

And Alice opened the parcel, and had her presence of mind by this time; and, amazed as she was at the gold shoes, showed no amazement,— nay, even slipped off her own slipper, and showed that the gold shoe fitted, to the delight of Tom, who was trying to explain that the man would change them if they were too small. She found an apple for each boy, thanked and praised each one separately; and the interview would have been perfect, had she not innocently asked Tom what was the matter with his eye. Tom's eye! Why, it was the black eye John Flagg gave him. I am sorry to say Bill Floyd sniggered; but Pat came to the front this time, and said "a man hurt him." Then Alice produced some mittens, which had been left, and asked whose those were. But the boys did not know.

"I say, fellars, I'm going down to the writing-school, at the Union," said Pat, when they got into the street, all of them being in the mood that conceals emotion. "I say, let's all go."

To this they agreed.

"I say, I went there last week Monday, with Meg McManus. I say, fellars, it's real good fun."

The other fellows, having on the unfamiliar best rig, were well aware that they must not descend to their familiar haunts, and all consented.

To the amazement of the teacher, these three hulking boys allied themselves to the side of order, took their places as they were bidden, turned the public opinion of the class, and made the Botany Bay of the school to be its quietest class that night.

To his amazement the same result followed the next night. And to his greater amazement, the next.

To Alice's amazement, she received on Twelfth Night a gilt valentine envelope, within which, on heavily ruled paper, were announced these truths:—

Marm,—The mitins wur Nora Killpatrick's. She lives inn Water street place behind the Lager Brewery.

Yours to command,
William Floyd.
Thomas Mulligan.
Patrick Crehore.

The names which they could copy from signs were correctly spelled.

To Pat's amazement, Tom Mulligan held on at the writing-school all winter. When it ended, he wrote the best hand of any of them.

To my amazement, one evening when I looked in at Longman's, two years to a day after Alice's tree, a bright black-eyed young man, who had tied up for me the copy of Masson's "Milton," which I had given myself for a Christmas present, said: "You don't remember me." I owned innocence.

"My name is Mulligan—Thomas Mulligan. Would you thank Mr. John Flagg, if you meet him, for a Christmas present he gave me two years ago, at Miss Alice MacNeil's Christmas-tree. It was the best present I ever had, and the only one I ever deserved."

And I said I would do so.

I told Alice afterward never to think she was going to catch all the fish there were in any school. I told her to whiten the water with ground-bait enough for all, and to thank God if her heavenly fishing were skilful enough to save one.

Daily Bread

CHAPTER I

A QUESTION OF NOURISHMENT

*A*nd how is he?" said Robert, as he came in from his day's work, in every moment of which he had thought of his child. He spoke in a whisper to his wife, who met him in the narrow entry at the head of the stairs. And in a whisper she replied.

"He is certainly no worse," said Mary: "the doctor says, maybe a shade better. At least," she said, sitting on the lower step, and holding her husband's hand, and still whispering,—"at least he said that the breathing seemed to him a shade easier, one lung seemed to him a little more free, and that it is now a question of time and nourishment."

"Nourishment?"

"Yes, nourishment,—and I own my heart sunk as he said so. Poor little thing, he loathes the slops, and I told the doctor so. I told him the struggle and fight to get them down his poor little throat gave him more flush and fever than any thing. And then he begged me not to try that again, asked if there were really nothing that the child would take, and suggested every thing so kindly. But the poor little thing, weak as he is, seems to rise up with supernatural strength against them all. I am not sure, though, but perhaps we may do something with the old milk and water: that is really my only hope now, and that is the reason I spoke to you so cheerfully."

Then poor Mary explained more at length that Emily had brought in Dr. Cummings's Manual[1] about the use of milk with children, and that they had sent round to the Corlisses', who always had good milk, and had set a pint according to the direction and formula,—and that though dear little Jamie had refused the groats and the barley, and I know not what else, that at six he had gladly taken all the watered milk they dared to give him, and that it now had rested on his stomach half an hour, so that she could not but hope that the tide had turned, only she hoped with trembling, because he had so steadily refused cow's milk only the week before.

This rapid review in her entry, of the bulletins of a day, is really the beginning of this Christmas story. No matter which day it was,—it was a little before Christmas, and one of the shortest days, but I have forgotten which. Enough that the baby, for he was a baby still, just entering his thirteenth month,—enough that he did relish the milk, so carefully measured

---

[1] Has the reader a delicate infant? Let him send for Dr. Cummings's little book on Milk for Children.

and prepared, and hour by hour took his little dole of it as if it had come from his mother's breast. Enough that three or four days went by so, the little thing lying so still on his back in his crib, his lips still so blue, and his skin of such deadly color against the white of his pillow, and that, twice a day, as Dr. Morton came in and felt his pulse, and listened to the panting, he smiled and looked pleased, and said, "We are getting on better than I dared expect." Only every time he said, "Does he still relish the milk?" and every time was so pleased to know that he took to it still, and every day he added a teaspoonful or two to the hourly dole,—and so poor Mary's heart was lifted day by day.

This lasted till St. Victoria's day. Do you know which day that is? It is the second day before Christmas; and here, properly speaking, the story begins.

CHAPTER II

ST. VICTORIA'S DAY

St. Victoria's day the doctor was full two hours late. Mary was not anxious about this. She was beginning to feel bravely about the boy, and no longer counted the minutes till she could hear the door-bell ring. When he came he loitered in the entry below,—or she thought he did. He was long coming up stairs. And when he came in she saw that he was excited by something,—was really even then panting for breath.

"I am here at last," he said. "Did you think I should fail you?"

Why, no,—poor innocent Mary had not thought any such thing. She had known he would come,—and baby was so well that she had not minded his delay.

Morton looked up at the close drawn shades, which shut out the light, and said, "You did not think of the storm?"

"Storm? no!" said poor Mary. She had noticed, when Robert went to the door at seven and she closed it after him, that some snow was falling. But she had not thought of it again. She had kissed him, told him to keep up good heart, and had come back to her baby.

Then the doctor told her that the storm which had begun before day-break had been gathering more and more severely; that the drifts were already heavier than he remembered them in all his Boston life; that after half an hour's trial in his sleigh he had been glad to get back to the stable with his horse; and that all he had done since he had done on foot, with difficulty she could not conceive of. He had been so long down stairs while he brushed the snow off, that he might be fit to come near the child.

"And really, Mrs. Walter, we are doing so well here," he said cheerfully, "that I will not try to come round this afternoon, unless you see a change. If you do, your husband must come up for me, you know. But you will not need me, I am sure."

Mary felt quite brave to think that they should not need him really for twenty-four hours, and said so; and added, with the first smile he had seen for a fortnight: "I do not know anybody to whom it is of less account than to me, whether the streets are blocked or open. Only I am sorry for you."

Poor Mary, how often she thought of that speech, before Christmas day went by! But she did not think of it all through St. Victoria's day. Her husband did not come home to dinner. She did not expect him. The children came from school at two, rejoicing in the long morning session and the half holiday of the afternoon which had been earned by it. They had some story of their frolic in the snow, and after dinner went quietly away to their little play-room in the attic. And Mary sat with her baby all the afternoon,—nor wanted other company. She could count his breathing now, and knew how to time it by the watch, and she knew that it was steadier and slower than it was the day before. And really he almost showed an appetite for the hourly dole. Her husband was not late. He had taken care of that, and had left the shop an hour early. And as he came in and looked at the child from the other side of the crib, and smiled so cheerfully on her, Mary felt that she could not enough thank God for his mercy.

CHAPTER III

ST. VICTORIA'S DAY IN THE COUNTRY

Five and twenty miles away was another mother, with a baby born the same day as Jamie. Mary had never heard of her and never has heard of her, and, unless she reads this story, never will hear of her till they meet together in the other home, look each other in the face, and know as they are known. Yet their two lives, as you shall see, are twisted together, as indeed are all lives, only they do not know it—as how should they?

A great day for Huldah Stevens was this St. Victoria's day. Not that she knew its name more than Mary did. Indeed it was only of late years that Huldah Stevens had cared much for keeping Christmas day. But of late years they had all thought of it more; and this year, on Thanksgiving day, at old Mr. Stevens's, after great joking about the young people's housekeeping, it had been determined, with some banter, that the same party should meet with John and Huldah on Christmas eve, with all Huldah's side of the house besides, to a late dinner or early supper, as the guests might please to call it. Little difference between the meals, indeed, was there ever in the profusion of these country homes. The men folks were seldom at home at the noon-day meal, call it what you will. For they were all in the milk-business, as you will see. And, what with collecting the milk from the hill-farms, on the one hand, and then carrying it for delivery at the three o'clock morning milk-train, on the other hand, any hours which you, dear reader, might consider systematic, or of course in country life, were certainly always set aside. But, after much conference, as I have said, it had been determined at the Thanksgiving party that all hands in both families should meet at John and Huldah's as near three o'clock as they could the day before Christmas; and then and there Huldah was to show her powers in entertaining at her first state family party.

So this St. Victoria's day was a great day of preparation for Huldah, if she had only known its name, as she did not. For she was of the kind which prepares in time, not of the kind that is caught out when the company come with the work half done. And as John started on his collection beat that morning at about the hour Robert, in town, kissed Mary good-by, Huldah stood on the step with him, and looked with satisfaction on the gathering snow, because it would make better sleighing the next day for her father and mother to come over. She charged him not to forget her box of raisins when he came back, and to ask at the express if anything came up from town, bade him good-by, and turned back into the house, not wholly dissatisfied to be almost alone. She washed her baby, gave him his first lunch and put him to bed. Then, with the coast fairly clear,—what woman does not enjoy a clear coast, if it only be early enough in the morning?—she dipped boldly and wisely into her flour-barrel, stripped her plump round arms to their work, and began on the pie-crust which was to appear to-morrow in the fivefold forms of apple, cranberry, Marlboro', mince, and squash,—care-ful and discriminating in the nice chemistry of her mixtures and the nice manipulations of her handicraft, but in nowise dreading the issue. A long, active, lively morning she had of it. Not dissatisfied with the stages of her work, step by step she advanced, stage by stage she attained of the elaborate plan which was well laid out in her head, but, of course, had never been intrusted to words, far less to tell-tale paper. From the oven at last came the pies,—and she was satisfied with the color; from the other oven came the turkey, which she proposed to have cold,—as a relay, or *pièce de résistance*, for any who might not be at hand at the right moment for dinner. Into the empty oven went the clove-blossoming ham, which, as it boiled, had given the least appetizing odor to the kitchen. In the pretty moulds in the wood-shed stood the translucent cranberry hardening to its fixed consistency. In other moulds the obedient calf's foot already announced its willingness and intention to "gell" as she directed. Huldah's decks were cleared again, her kitchen table fit to cut out "work" upon,—all the pans and plates were put away, which accumulate so mysteriously where cooking is going forward; on its nail hung the weary jigger, on its hook the spicy grater, on the roller a fresh towel. Everything gave sign of victory, the whole kitchen looking only a little nicer than usual. Huldah herself was dressed for the afternoon, and so was the baby; and nobody but as acute observers as you and I would have known that she had been in action all along the line and had won the battle at every point, when two o'clock came, the earliest moment at which her husband ever returned.

Then for the first time it occurred to Huldah to look out doors and see how fast the snow was gathering. She knew it was still falling. But the storm was a quiet one, and she had had too much to do to be gaping out of the windows. She went to the shed door, and to her amazement saw that the north wood-pile was wholly drifted in! Nor could she, as she stood, see the fences of the roadway!

Huldah ran back into the house, opened the parlor door and drew up the curtain, to see that there were indeed no fences on the front of the house to be seen. On the northwest, where the wind had full sweep,—between her and the barn, the ground was bare. But all that snow—and who should say how much more?—was piled up in front of her; so that unless Huldah had known every landmark, she would not have suspected that any road was ever there. She looked uneasily out at the northwest windows, but she could not see an inch to windward: dogged snow—snow—snow—as if it would never be done.

Huldah knew very well then that there was no husband for her in the next hour, nor most like in the next or the next. She knew very well too what she had to do; and, knowing it, she did it. She tied on her hood, and buttoned tight around her her rough sack, passed through the shed and crossed that bare strip to the barn, opened the door with some difficulty, because snow was already drifting into the doorway, and entered. She gave the cows and oxen their water and the two night horses theirs,—went up into the loft and pitched down hay enough for all,—went down stairs to the pigs and cared for them,—took one of the barn shovels and cleared a path where she had had to plunge into the snow at the doorway, took the shovel back, and then crossed home again to her baby. She thought she saw the Empsons' chimney smoking as she went home, and that seemed companionable. She took off her over-shoes, sack, and hood, said aloud, "This will be a good stay-at-home day," brought round her desk to the kitchen table, and began on a nice long letter to her brother Cephas in Seattle.

That letter was finished, eight good quarto pages written, and a long delayed letter to Emily Tabor, whom Huldah had not seen since she was married; and a long pull at her milk accounts had brought them up to date,—and still no John. Huldah had the table all set, you may be sure of that; but, for herself, she had had no heart to go through the formalities of lunch or dinner. A cup of tea and something to eat with it as she wrote did better, she thought, for her,—and she could eat when the men came. It is a way women have. Not till it became quite dark, and she set her kerosene lamp in the window that he might have a chance to see it when he turned the Locust Grove corner, did Huldah once feel herself lonely, or permit herself to wish that she did not live in a place where she could be cut off from all her race. "If John had gone into partnership with Joe Winter and we had lived in Boston." This was the thought that crossed her mind. Dear Huldah,—from the end of one summer to the beginning of the next, Joe Winter does not go home to his dinner; and what you experience to-day, so far as absence from your husband goes, is what his wife experiences in Boston ten months, save Sundays, in every year.

I do not mean that Huldah winced or whined. Not she. Only she did think "if." Then she sat in front of the stove and watched the coals, and for a little while continued to think "if." Not long. Very soon she was engaged in planning how she would arrange the table to-morrow,—whether Mother Stevens should cut the chicken-pie, or whether she would have that in front of her own mother. Then she fell to planning what she would make for Cynthia's baby,—and then to wondering whether Cephas was in earnest in that half nonsense he wrote about Sibyl Dyer,—and then the clock struck six!

No bells yet,—no husband,—no anybody. Lantern out and lighted. Rubber boots on, hood and sack. Shed-shovel in one hand, lantern in the other. Roadway still bare, but a drift as high as Huldah's shoulders at the barn door. Lantern on the ground; snow-shovel in both hands now. One, two, three!—one cubic foot out. One, two, three!—another cubic foot out. And so on, and so on, and so on, till the doorway is clear again. Lantern in one hand, snow-shovel in the other, we enter the barn, draw the water for cows and oxen,—we shake down more hay, and see to the pigs again. This time we make beds of straw for the horses and the cattle. Nay, we linger a minute or two, for there is something companionable there. Then we shut them in, in the dark, and cross the well-cleared roadway to the shed, and so home again. Certainly Mrs. Empson's kerosene lamp is in her window. That must be her light which gives a little halo in that direction in the falling snow. That looks like society.

And this time Huldah undresses the baby, puts on her yellow flannel night-gown,—makes the whole as long as it may be,—and then, still making believe be jolly, lights another lamp, eats her own supper, clears it away, and cuts into the new Harper which John had brought up to her the day before.

But the Harper is dull reading to her, though generally so attractive. And when her Plymouth-Hollow clock consents to strike eight at last,

Huldah, who has stinted herself to read till eight, gladly puts down the "Travels in Arizona," which seem to her as much like the "Travels in Peru," of the month before, as those had seemed like the "Travels in Chinchilla." Rubber boots again,—lantern again,—sack and hood again. The men will be in no case for milking when they come. So Huldah brings together their pails,—takes her shovel once more and her lantern,—digs out the barn drift again, and goes over to milk little Carry and big Fanchon. For, though the milking of a hundred cows passes under those roofs and out again every day, Huldah is far too conservative to abandon the custom which she inherits from some Thorfinn or some Elfrida, and her husband is well pleased to humor her in keeping in that barn always, at least two of the choicest three-quarter blood cows that he can choose, for the family supply. Only, in general, he or Reuben milks them; as duties are divided there, this is not Huldah's share. But on this eve of St. Spiridion the gentle creatures were glad when she came in; and in two journeys back and forth Huldah had carried her well-filled pails into her dairy. This helped along the hour, and just after nine o'clock struck, she could hear the cheers of the men at last. She ran out again with the ready lighted lantern to the shed-door,—in an instant had on her boots and sack and hood, had crossed to the barn, and slid open the great barn door,—and stood there with her light,—another Hero for another Leander to buffet towards, through the snow. A sight to see were the two men, to be sure! And a story, indeed, they had to tell! On their different beats they had fought snow all day, had been breaking roads with the help of the farmers where they could, had had to give up more than half of the outlying farms, sending such messages as they might, that the outlying farmers might bring down to-morrow's milk to such stations as they could arrange, and, at last, by good luck, had both met at the dépôt in the hollow, where each had gone to learn at what hour the milk-train might be expected in the morning. Little reason was there, indeed, to expect it at all. Nothing had passed the station-master since the morning express, called lightning by satire, had slowly pushed up with three or four engines five hours behind its time, and just now had come down a messenger from them that he should telegraph to Boston that they were all blocked up at Tyler's Summit,—the snow drifting beneath their wheels faster than they could clear it. Above, the station-master said, nothing whatever had yet passed Winchendon. Five engines had gone out from Fitchburg eastward, but in the whole day they had not come as far as Leominster. It was very clear that no milk-train nor any other train would be on time the next morning.

Such was, in brief, John's report to Huldah, when they had got to that state of things in which a man can make a report; that is, after they had rubbed dry the horses, had locked up the barn, after the men had rubbed themselves dry, and had put on dry clothing, and after each of them, sitting on the fire side of the table, had drunk his first cup of tea, and eaten his first square cubit of dipped-toast. After the dipped-toast, they were going to begin on Huldah's fried potatoes and sausages.

Huldah heard their stories with all their infinite little details; knew every corner and turn by which they had husbanded strength and life; was grateful to the Corbetts and Varnums and Prescotts and the rest, who, with their oxen and their red right hands, had given such loyal help for the common good; and she heaved a deep sigh when the story ended with the verdict of the failure of the whole,—"No trains on time to-morrow."

"Bad for the Boston babies," said Reuben bluntly, giving words to what the others were feeling. "Poor little things!" said Huldah, "Alice has been so pretty all day." And she gulped down just one more sigh, disgusted with herself, as she remembered that "if" of the afternoon,—"if John had only gone into partnership with Joe Winter."

CHAPTER IV

HOW THEY BROKE THE BLOCKADE

Three o'clock in the morning saw Huldah's fire burning in the stove, her water boiling in the kettle, her slices of ham broiling on the grid-iron, and quarter-past three saw the men come across from the barn, where they had been shaking down hay for the cows and horses, and yoking the oxen for the terrible onset of the day. It was bright star-light above,— thank Heaven for that. This strip of three hundred thousand square miles of snow cloud, which had been drifting steadily cast over a continent, was, it seemed, only twenty hours wide,—say two hundred miles, more or less,—and at about midnight its last flecks had fallen, and all the heaven was washed black and clear. The men were well rested by those five hours of hard sleep. They were fitly dressed for their great encounter and started cheerily upon it, as men who meant to do their duty, and to both of whom, indeed, the thought had come, that life and death might be trembling in their hands. They did not take out the pungs to-day, nor, of course, the horses. Such milk as they had collected on St. Victoria's day they had stored already at the station, and at Stacy's; and the best they could do to-day would be to break open the road from the Four Corners to the station, that they might place as many cans as possible there before the down-train came. From the house, then, they had only to drive down their oxen that they might work with the other teams from the Four Corners; and it was only by begging him, that Huldah persuaded Reuben to take one lunch-can for them both. Then, as Reuben left the door, leaving John to kiss her "good-by," and to tell her not to be alarmed if they did not come home at night,—she gave to John the full milk-can into which she had poured every drop of Carry's milk, and said, "It will be one more; and God knows what child may be crying for it now."

So they parted for eight and twenty hours; and in place of Huldah's first state party of both families, she and Alice reigned solitary that day, and held their little court with never a suitor. And when her lunch-time came, Huldah looked half-mournfully, half-merrily, on her array of dainties prepared for the feast, and she would not touch one of them. She toasted some bread before the fire, made a cup of tea, boiled an egg, and would not so much as set the table. As has been before stated, this is the way with women.

And of the men, who shall tell the story of the pluck and endurance, of the unfailing good-will, of the resource in strange emergency, of the mutual help and common courage with which all the men worked that day on that well-nigh hopeless task of breaking open the highway from the Corners to the station? Well-nigh hopeless, indeed; for although at first, with fresh cattle and united effort, they made in the hours, which passed so quickly up to ten o'clock, near two miles headway, and had brought yesterday's milk thus far,—more than half way to their point of delivery,—at ten o'clock it was quite evident that this sharp northwest wind, which told so heavily on the oxen and even on the men, was filling in the very roadway they had opened, and so was cutting them off from their base, and, by its new drifts, was leaving the roadway for to-day's milk even worse than it was when they began. In one of those extemporized councils, then,—such as fought the battle of Bunker Hill, and threw the tea into Boston harbor,—it was determined, at ten o'clock, to divide the working parties. The larger body should work back to the Four Corners, and by proper relays keep that trunk line of road open, if they could; while six yoke, with their owners, still pressing forward to the station, should make a new base at Lovejoy's, where, when these oxen gave out, they could be put up at his barn. It was quite clear, indeed, to the experts that that time was not far distant.

And so, indeed, it proved. By three in the afternoon, John and Reuben and the other leaders of the advance party—namely, the whole of it, for such is the custom of New England—gathered around the fire at Lovejoy's, conscious that after twelve hours of such battle as Pavia never saw, nor Roncesvalles, they were defeated at every point but one. Before them the mile of road which they had made in the steady work of hours was drifted in again as smooth as the surrounding pastures, only if possible a little more treacherous for the labor which they had thrown away upon it. The oxen which had worked kindly and patiently, well handled by good-tempered men, yet all confused and half dead with exposure, could do no more. Well, indeed, if those that had been stalled fast, and had had to stand in that biting wind after gigantic effort, escaped with their lives from such exposure. All that the men had gained was that they had advanced their first dépôt of milk—two hundred and thirty-nine cans—as far as Lovejoy's. What supply might have worked down to the Four Corners behind them, they did not know and hardly cared, their communications that way being well-nigh cut off again. What they thought of, and planned for, was simply how these cans at Lovejoy's could be put on any downward train. For by this time they knew that all trains would have lost their grades and their names, and that this milk would go into Boston by the first engine that went there, though it rode on the velvet of a palace car.

What train this might be, they did not know. From the hill above Lovejoy's they could see poor old Dix, the station-master, with his wife and boys, doing his best to make an appearance of shovelling in front of his little station. But Dix's best was but little, for he had but one arm, having lost the other in a collision, and so as a sort of pension the company had placed him at this little flag-station, where was a roof over his head, a few tickets to sell, and generally very little else to do. It was clear enough that no working parties on the railroad had worked up to Dix, or had worked down; nor was it very likely that any would before night, unless the railroad people had better luck with their drifts than our friends had found. But, as to this, who should say? Snow-drifts are "mighty onsartain." The line of that road is in general northwest, and to-day's wind might have cleaned out its gorges as persistently as it had filled up our crosscuts. From Lovejoy's barn they could see that the track was now perfectly clear for the half mile where it crossed the Prescott meadows.

I am sorry to have been so long in describing thus the aspect of the field after the first engagement. But it was on this condition of affairs that, after full conference, the enterprises of the night were determined. Whatever was to be done was to be done by men. And after thorough regale on Mrs. Lovejoy's green tea, and continual return to her constant relays of thin bacon gilded by unnumbered eggs; after cutting and coming again upon unnumbered mince-pies, which, I am sorry to say, did not in any point compare well with Huldah's,—each man thrust many doughnuts into his outside pockets, drew on the long boots again, and his buckskin gloves and mittens, and, unencumbered now by the care of animals, started on the work of the evening. The sun was just taking his last look at them from the western hills, where Reuben and John could see Huldah's chimney smoking. The plan was, by taking a double hand-sled of Lovejoy's, and by knocking together two or three more, jumper-fashion, to work their way across the meadow to the railroad causeway, and establish a milk dépôt there, where the line was not half a mile from Lovejoy's. By going and coming often, following certain tracks well known to Lovejoy on the windward side of walls and fences, these eight men felt quite sure that by midnight they could place all their milk at the spot where the old farm crossing strikes the railroad. Meanwhile, Silas Lovejoy, a boy of fourteen, was to put on a pair of snow-shoes, go down to the station, state the case to old Dix, and get from him a red lantern and permission to stop the first train where it swept out from the Pitman cut upon the causeway. Old Dix had no more right to give this permission than had the humblest street-sweeper in Ispahan, and this they all knew. But the fact that Silas had asked for it would show a willingness on their part to submit to authority, if authority there had been. This satis-fied the New England love of law, on the one hand. On the other hand, the train would be stopped, and this satisfied the New England determination to get the thing done any way. To give additional force to Silas, John pro-vided him with a note to Dix, and it was generally agreed that if Dix wasn't ugly, he would give the red lantern and the permission. Silas was then to work up the road and station himself as far beyond the curve as he could, and stop the first down-train. He was to tell the conductor where the men were waiting with the milk, was to come down to them on the train, and his duty would be done. Lest Dix should be ugly, Silas was provided with Lovejoy's only lantern, but he was directed not to show this at the station until his interview was finished. Silas started cheerfully on his snow-shoes; John and Lovejoy, at the same time, starting with the first hand-sled of the cans. First of all into the sled, John put Huldah's well-known can, a little shorter than the others, and with a different handle. "Whatever else went to Boston," he said, "that can was bound to go through."

They established the basis of their pyramid, and met the three new jumpers with their makers as they went back for more. This party enlarged the base of the pyramid; and, as they worked, Silas passed them cheerfully with his red lantern. Old Dix had not been ugly, had given the lantern and all the permission he had to give, and had communicated some intelligence also. The intelligence was, that an accumulated force of seven engines, with a large working party, had left Groton Junction downward at three. Nothing had arrived upward at Groton Junction; and, from Boston, Dix learned that nothing more would leave there till early morning. No trains had arrived in Boston from any quarter for twenty-four hours. So long the blockade had lasted already.

On this intelligence, it was clear that, with good luck, the down-train might reach them at any moment. Still the men resolved to leave their milk, while they went back for more, relying on Silas and the "large work-ing party" to put it on the cars, if the train chanced to pass before any of them returned. So back they fared to Lovejoy's for their next relay, and met John and Reuben working in successfully with their second. But no one need have hurried; for, as trip after trip they built their pyramid of cans higher and higher, no welcome whistle broke the stillness of the night, and by ten o'clock, when all these cans were in place by the rail, the train had not yet come.

John and Reuben then proposed to go up into the cut, and to relieve poor Silas, who had not been heard from since he swung along so cheerfully like an "Excelsior" boy on his way up the Alps. But they had hardly started, when a horn from the meadow recalled them, and, retracing their way, they met a messenger who had come in to say that a fresh team from the Four Corners had been reported at Lovejoy's, with a dozen or more men, who had succeeded in bringing down nearly as far as Lovejoy's mowing-lot near a hundred more cans; that it was quite possible in two or three hours more to bring this over also,—and, although the first train was probably now close at hand, it was clearly worth while to place this relief in readiness for a second. So poor Silas was left for the moment to his loneliness, and Reuben and John returned again upon their steps. They passed the house where they found Mrs. Lovejoy and Mrs. Stacy at work in the shed, finishing off two more jumpers, and claiming congratulation for their skill, and after a cup of tea again,—for no man touched spirit that day nor that night,—they reported at the new station by the mowing-lot.

And Silas Lovejoy—who had turned the corner into the Pitman cut, and so shut himself out from sight of the station light, or his father's windows, or the lanterns of the party at the pyramid of cans—Silas Lovejoy held his watch there, hour by hour, with such courage as the sense of the advance gives boy or man. He had not neglected to take the indispensable shovel as he came. In going over the causeway he had slipped off the snow-shoes and hung them on his back. Then there was heavy wading as he turned into the Pitman cut, knee deep, middle deep, and he laid his snow-shoes on the snow and set the red lantern on them, as he reconnoitred. Middle deep, neck deep, and he fell forward on his face into the yielding mass. "This will not do, I must not fall like that often," said Silas to himself, as he gained his balance and threw himself backward against the mass. Slowly he turned round, worked back to the lantern, worked out to the causeway, and fastened on the shoes again. With their safer help he easily skimmed up to Pitman's bridge, which he had determined on for his station. He knew that thence his lantern could be seen for a mile, and that yet there the train might safely be stopped, so near was the open causeway which he had just traversed. He had no fear of an up-train behind him.

So Silas walked back and forth, and sang, and spouted "pieces," and mused on the future of his life, and spouted "pieces" again, and sang in the loneliness. How the time passed, he did not know. No sound of clock, no baying of dog, no plash of waterfall, broke that utter stillness. The wind, thank God, had at last died away; and Silas paced his beat in a long oval he made for himself, under and beyond the bridge, with no sound but his own voice when he chose to raise it. He expected, as they all did, that every moment the whistle of the train, as it swept into sight a mile or more away, would break the silence; so he paced, and shouted, and sang.

"This is a man's duty," he said to himself: "they would not let me go with the fifth regiment,—not as a drummer boy; but this is duty such as no drummer boy of them all is doing. Company, march!" and he "stepped forward smartly" with his left foot. "Really I am placed on guard here quite as much as if I were on picket in Virginia." "Who goes there?" "Advance, friend, and give the countersign." Not that any one did go there, or could go there; but the boy's fancy was ready, and so he amused himself during the first hours. Then he began to wonder whether they were hours, as they seemed, or whether this was all a wretched illusion,—that the time passed slowly to him because he was nothing but a boy, and did not know how to occupy his mind. So he resolutely said the multiplication-table from the beginning to the end, and from the end to the beginning,—first to himself, and again aloud, to make it slower. Then he tried the ten commandments. "Thou shalt have none other Gods before me:" easy to say that beneath those stars; and he said them again. No, it is no illusion. I must have been here hours long! Then he began on Milton's hymn:—

> "It was the winter wild,
> While the heaven-born child,
> All meanly wrapt, in the rude manger lies."

"Winter wild, indeed," said Silas aloud; and, if he had only known it, at that moment the sun beneath his feet was crossing the meridian, midnight had passed already, and Christmas day was born!

> "Only with speeches fair
> She wooes the gentle air
> To hide her guilty front with innocent snow."

"Innocent, indeed," said poor Silas, still aloud, "much did he know of innocent snow!" And vainly did he try to recall the other stanzas, as he paced back and forth, round and round, and began now to wonder where his father and the others were, and if they could have come to any misfortune. Surely, they could not have forgotten that he was here. Would that train never come?

If he were not afraid of its coming at once, he would have run back to the causeway to look for their lights,—and perhaps they had a fire. Why had he not brought an axe for a fire? "That rail fence above would have served perfectly,—nay, it is not five rods to a load of hickory we left the day before Thanksgiving. Surely one of them might come up to me with an axe. But maybe there is trouble below. They might have come with an axe—with an axe—with an axe—with an—axe"—"I am going to sleep," cried Silas,—aloud again this time,—as his head dropped heavily on the handle of the shovel he was resting on there in the lee of the stone wall. "I am going to sleep,— that will never do. Sentinel asleep at his post. Order out the relief. Blind his eyes. Kneel, sir. Make ready. Fire. That, sir, for sentinels asleep." And so Silas laughed grimly, and began his march again. Then he took his shovel and began a great pit where he supposed the track might be beneath him. "Anything to keep warm and to keep awake. But why did they not send up to him? Why was he here? Why was he all alone? He who had never been alone before. Was he alone? Was there companionship in the stars,—or in the good God who held the stars? Did the good God put me here? If he put me here, will he keep me here? Or did he put me here to die! To die in this cold? It is cold,—it is very cold ! Is there any good in my dying? The train will run down, and they will see a dead body lying under the bridge,—black on the snow, with a red lantern by it. Then they will stop. Shall I—I will— just go back to see if the lights are at the bend. I will leave the lantern here on the edge of this wall!" And so Silas turned, half benumbed, worked his way nearly out of the gorge, and started as he heard, or thought he heard, a baby's scream. "A thousand babies are starving, and I am afraid to stay here to give them their life," he said. "There is a boy fit for a soldier! Order out the relief! Drum-head court-martial! Prisoner, hear your sentence! Deserter, to be shot! Blindfold,—kneel, sir! Fire! Good enough for deserters!" And so poor Silas worked back again to the lantern.

And now he saw and felt sure that Orion was bending downward, and he knew that the night must be broken; and, with some new hope, throwing down the shovel with which he had been working, he began his soldier tramp once more,—as far as soldier tramp was possible with those trailing snow-shoes,—tried again on "No war nor battle sound," broke down on "Cynthia's seat" and the "music of the spheres;" but at last,—working on "beams," "long beams," and "that with long beams,"—he caught the stanzas he was feeling for, and broke out exultant with,—

> "At last surrounds their sight,
>   A globe of circular light
> That with long beams the shame-faced night arrayed;
>   The helmed cherubim
>   And sworded seraphim
> Are seen in glittering ranks—"

"Globe of circular light—am I dreaming, or have they come!"—

Come they had! The globe of circular light swept full over the valley, and the scream of the engine was welcomed by the freezing boy as if it had been an angel's whisper to him. Not unprepared did it find him. The red lantern swung to and fro in a well-practised hand, and he was in waiting on his firmest spot as the train *slowed* and the engine passed him.

"Do not stop for me," he cried, as he threw his weight heavily on the tender side, and the workmen dragged him in. "Only run slow till you are out of the ledge: we have made a milk station at the cross-road."

"Good for you!" said the wondering fireman, who in a moment understood the exigency. The heavy plough threw out the snow steadily still, in ten seconds they were clear of the ledge, and saw the fire-light shimmering on the great pyramids of milk-cans. Slower and slower ran the train, and by the blazing fire stopped, for once, because its masters chose to stop. And the working party on the train cheered lustily as they tumbled out of the cars, as they apprehended the situation, and were cheered by the working party from the village.

Two or three cans of milk stood on the embers of the fire, that they might be ready for the men on the train with something that was at least warm. An empty passenger car was opened and the pyramids of milk-cans were hurried into it,—forty men now assisting.

"You will find Joe Winter at the Boston station," said John Stevens to the "gentlemanly conductor" of the express, whose lightning train had thus become a milk convoy. "Tell Winter to distribute this among all the carts, that everybody may have some. Good luck to you. Good-by!" And the engines snorted again, and John Stevens turned back, not so much as thinking that he had made his Christmas present to a starving town.

CHAPTER V

CHRISTMAS MORNING

The children were around Robert Walter's knees, and each of the two spelled out a verse of the second chapter of Luke, on Christmas morning. And Robert and Mary kneeled with them, and they said together, "Our Father who art in heaven." Mary's voice broke a little when they came to "daily bread," but with the two, and her husband, she continued to the end, and could say "thine is the power," and believe it too.

"Mamma," whispered little Fanny, as she kissed her mother after the prayer, "when I said my prayer up stairs last night, I said 'our daily milk,' and so did Robert." This was more than poor Mary could bear. She kissed the child, and she hurried away.

For last night at six o'clock it was clear that the milk was sour, and little Jamie had detected it first of all. Then, with every one of the old wiles, they had gone back over the old slops; but the child, with that old weird strength, had pushed them all away. Christmas morning broke, and poor Robert, as soon as light would serve, had gone to the neighbors all,—their nearest intimates they had tried the night before,—and from all had brought back the same reply; one friend had sent a wretched sample, but the boy detected the taint and pushed it, untasted, away. Dr. Morton had the alarm the day before. He was at the house earlier than usual with some condensed milk, which his wife's stores had furnished; but that would not answer. Poor Jamie pushed this by. There was some smoke or something,—who should say what?—it would not do. The doctor could see in an instant how his patient had fallen back in the night. That weird, anxious, entreating look, as his head lay back on the little pillow, had all come back again. Robert and Robert's friends, Gaisford and Warren, had gone down to the Old Colony, to the Worcester, and to the Hartford stations. Perhaps their trains were doing better. The door-bell rang yet again. "Mrs. Appleton's love to Mrs. Walter, and perhaps her child will try some fresh beef-tea." As if poor Jamie did not hate beef-tea; still Morton resolutely forced three spoonfuls down. Half an hour more and Mrs. Dudley's compliments. "Mrs. Dudley heard that Mrs. Walter was out of milk, and took the liberty to send round some very particularly nice Scotch groats, which her brother had just brought from Edinburgh." "Do your best with it, Fanny," said poor Mary, but she knew that if Jamie took those Scotch groats it was only because they were a Christmas present. Half an hour more! Three more spoonfuls of beef-tea after a fight. Door-bell again. Carriage at the door. "Would Mrs. Walter come down and see Mrs. Fitch? It was really very particular." Mary was half dazed, and went down, she did not know why.

"Dear Mrs. Walter, you do not remember me," said this eager girl, crossing the room and taking her by both hands.

"Why, no—yes—do I?" said Mary, crying and laughing together.

"Yes, you will remember, it was at church, at the baptism. My Jennie and your Jamie were christened the same day. And now I hear,—we all know how low he is,—and perhaps he will share my Jennie's breakfast. Dear Mrs. Walter, do let me try."

Then Mary saw that the little woman's cloak and hat were already thrown off,—which had not seemed strange to her before,—and the two passed quietly up stairs together; and Julia Fitch bent gently over him, and cooed to him, and smiled to him, but could not make the poor child smile. And they lifted him so gently on the pillow,—but only to hear him scream. And she brought his head gently to her heart, and drew back the little curtain that was left, and offered to him her life; but he was frightened, and did not know her, and had forgotten what it was she gave him, and screamed again; and so they had to lay him back gently upon the pillow. And then,—as Julia was saying she would stay, and how they could try again, and could do this and that,—then the door-bell rang again, and Mrs. Coleman had herself come round with a little white pitcher, and herself ran up stairs with it, and herself knocked at the door!

The blockade was broken, and

The milk had come!

Mary never knew that it was from Huldah Stevens's milk-can that her boy drank in the first drop of his new life. Nor did Huldah know it. Nor did John know it, nor the paladins who fought that day at his side. Nor did Silas Lovejoy know it.

But the good God and all good angels knew it. Why ask for more?

And you and I, dear reader, if we can forget that always our daily bread comes to us, because a thousand brave men and a thousand brave women are at work in the world, praying to God and trying to serve him, we will not forget it as we meet at breakfast on this blessed Christmas day!

Stand and Wait

CHAPTER I

CHRISTMAS EVE

"They've come! they've come!"

This was the cry of little Herbert as he ran in from the square stone which made the large doorstep of the house. Here he had been watching, a self-posted sentinel, for the moment when the carriage should turn the corner at the bottom of the hill.

"They've come! they've come!" echoed joyfully through the house; and the cry penetrated out into the extension, or ell, in which the grown members of the family were, in the kitchen, "getting tea" by some formulas more solemn than ordinary.

"Have they come?" cried Grace; and she set her skillet back to the quarter-deck, or after-part of the stove, lest its white contents should burn while she was away. She threw a waiting handkerchief over her shoulders, and ran with the others to the front door, to wave something white, and to be in at the first welcome.

Young and old were gathered there in that hospitable open space where the side road swept up to the barn on its way from the main road. The bigger boys of the home party had scattered half-way down the hill by this time. Even grandmamma had stepped down from the stone, and walked half-way to the roadway. Every one was waving something. Those who had no handkerchiefs had hats or towels to wave; and the more advanced boys began an undefined or irregular cheer.

But the carryall advanced slowly up the hill, with no answering handkerchief, and no bonneted head stretched out from the side. And, as it neared Sam and Andrew, their enthusiasm could be seen to droop, and George and Herbert stopped their cheers as it came up to them; and before it was near the house, on its grieved way up the hill, the bad news had come up before it, as bad news will,—"She has not come, after all."

It was Huldah Root, Grace's older sister, who had not come. John Root, their father, had himself driven down to the station to meet her; and Abner, her oldest brother, had gone with him. It was two years since she had been at home, and the whole family was on tiptoe to welcome her. Hence the unusual tea preparation; hence the sentinel on the doorstep; hence the general assembly in the yard; and, after all, she had not come! It was a wretched disappointment. Her mother had that heavy, silent look, which children take as the heaviest affliction of all, when they see it in their mother's faces. John Root himself led the horse into the barn, as if he did not care now for anything which might happen in heaven above or in earth beneath. The boys were voluble in their rage: "It is too bad!" and, "Grandmamma, don't you think it is too bad?" and, "It is the meanest thing I ever heard of in all my life!" and, "Grace, why don't you say anything? did you ever know anything so mean?" As for poor Grace herself, she was quite beyond saying anything. All the treasured words she had laid up to say to Huldah; all the doubts and hopes and guesses, which were secret to all but God, but which were to be poured out in Huldah's ear as soon as they were alone, were coming up one by one, as if to choke her. She had waited so long for this blessed fortnight of sympathy, and now she had lost it. Grace could say nothing. And poor grandmamma, on whom fell the stilling of the boys, was at heart as wretched as any of them.

Somehow, something got itself put on the supper-table; and, when John Root and Abner came in from the barn, they all sat down to pretend to eat something. What a miserable contrast to the Christmas eve party which had been expected!

The observance of Christmas is quite a novelty in the heart of New England among the lords of the manor. Winslow and Brewster, above Plymouth Rock, celebrated their first Christmas by making all hands work all day in the raising of their first house. It was in that way that a Christian empire was begun. They builded better than they knew. They and theirs, in that hard day's work, struck the key-note for New England for two centuries and a half. And many and many a New Englander, still in middle life, remembers that in childhood, though nurtured in Christian homes, he could not have told, if he were asked, on what day of the year Christmas fell. But as New England, in the advance of the world, has come into the general life of the world, she has shown no inaptitude for the greater enjoyments of life; and, with the true catholicity of her great Congregational system, her people and her churches seize, one after another, all the noble traditions of the loftiest memories. And so in this matter we have in hand; it happened that the Roots, in their hillside home, had determined that they would celebrate Christmas, as never had Roots done before since Josiah Root landed at Salem, from the "Hercules," with other Kentish people, in 1635. Abner and Gershom had cut and trimmed a pretty fir-balsam from the edge of the Hotchkiss clearing; and it was now in the best parlor. Grace, with Mary Bickford, her firm ally and other self, had gilded nuts, and rubbed lady apples, and strung popped corn; and the tree had been dressed in secret, the youngsters all locked and warned out from the room. The choicest turkeys of the drove, and the tenderest geese from the herd, and the plumpest fowls from the barnyard, had been sacrificed on consecrated altars. And all this was but as accompaniment and side illustration of the great glory of the celebration, which was, that Huldah, after her two years' absence,—Huldah was to come home.

And now she had not come,—nay, was not coming!

As they sat down at their Barmecide feast, how wretched the assemblage of unrivalled dainties seemed! John Root handed to his wife their daughter's letter; she read it, and gave it to Grace, who read it, and gave it to her grandmother. No one read it aloud. To read aloud in such trials is not the custom of New England.

BOSTON, DEC. 24, 1848.

Dear Father and Mother,—It is dreadful to disappoint you all, but I cannot come. I am all ready, and this goes by the carriage that was to take me to the cars. But our dear little Horace has just been brought home, I am afraid, dying; but we cannot tell, and I cannot leave him. You know there is really no one who can do what I can. He was riding on his pony. First the pony came home alone; and, in five minutes after, two policemen brought the dear child in a carriage. His poor mother is very calm, but cannot think yet, or do anything. We have sent for his father, who is down town. I try to hope that he may come to himself; but he only lies and draws long breaths on his little bed. The doctors are with him now; and I write this little scrawl to say how dreadfully sorry I am. A merry Christmas to you all. Do not be troubled about me.

YOUR OWN LOVING

—HULDAH

P.S. I have got some little presents for the children; but they are all in my trunk, and I cannot get them out now. I will make a bundle Monday. Good-by. The man is waiting.

This was the letter that was passed from hand to hand, of which the contents slowly trickled into the comprehension of all parties, according as their several ages permitted them to comprehend. Sam, as usual, broke the silence by saying,—

"It is a perfect shame! She might as well be a nigger slave! I suppose they think they have bought her and sold her. I should like to see 'em all, just for once, and tell 'em that her flesh and blood is as good as theirs; and that, with all their airs and their money, they've no business to"—

"Sam," said poor Grace, "you shall not say such things. Huldah has stayed because she chose to stay; and that is the worst of it. She will not think of herself, not for one minute; and so—everything happens."

And Grace was sobbing beyond speech again; and her intervention amounted, therefore, to little or nothing. The boys, through the evening, descanted among themselves on the outrage. Grandmamma, and at last their mother, took successive turns in taming their indignation; but, for all this, it was a miserable evening. As for John Root, he took a lamp in one hand, and "The Weekly Tribune" in the other, and sat before the fire, and pretended to read; but not once did John Root change the fold of the paper that evening. It was a wretched Christmas eve; and, at half-past eight, every light was out, and every member of the household was lying stark awake, in bed.

Huldah Root, you see, was a servant with the Bartletts, in Boston. When she was only sixteen, she was engaged at her "trade," as a vest-maker, in that town; and, by some chance, made an appointment to sew as a seamstress at Mrs. Bartlett's for a fortnight. There were any number of children to be clothed there; and the fortnight extended to a month. Then the month became two months. She grew fond of Mrs. Bartlett, because Mrs. Bartlett grew fond of her. The children adored her; and she kept an eye to them; and it ended in her engaging to spend the winter there, half-seamstress, half-nurse, half-nursery-governess, and a little of everything. From such a beginning, it had happened that she had lived there six years, in confidential service. She could cook better than any-body in the house,—better than Mrs. Bartlett herself; but it was not often that she tried her talent there. On a birthday perhaps, in August, she would make huckleberry cakes, by the old homestead "receipt," for the children. She had the run of all their clothes as nobody else did; took the younger ones to be measured; and saw that none of the older ones went out with a crack in a seam, or a rough edge at the foot of a trowser. It was whispered that Minnie had rather go into the sewing-room to get Huldah to "show her" about "alligation" or "square-root," than to wait for Miss Thurber's explanations in the morning. In fifty such ways, it happened that Huldah—who, on the roll-call of the census-man, probably rated as a nursery-maid in the house—was the confidential friend of every member of the family, from Mr. Bartlett, who wanted to know where "The Intelligencer" was, down to the chore-boy who came in to black the shoes. And so it was, that, when poor little Horace was brought in with his skull knocked in by the pony, Huldah was—and modestly knew that she was—the most essential person in the stunned family circle.

While her brothers and sisters were putting out their lights at New Durham, heart-sick and wounded, Huldah was sitting in that still room, where only the rough broken breathing of poor Horace broke the sound. She was changing, once in ten minutes, the ice-water cloths; was feeling of his feet sometimes; wetting his tongue once or twice in an hour; putting her finger to his pulse with a native sense, which needed no second-hand to help it; and all the time, with the thought of him, was remembering how grieved and hurt and heart-broken they were at home. Every half-hour or less, a pale face appeared at the door; and Huldah just slid across the room, and said, "He is really doing nicely, pray lie down;" or, "His pulse is surely better, I will certainly come to you if it flags;" or "Pray trust me, I will not let you wait a moment if he needs you;" or, "Pray get ready for to-morrow. An hour's sleep now will be worth everything to you then." And the poor mother would crawl back to her baby and her bed, and pretend to try to sleep; and in half an hour would appear again at the door. One o'clock, two o'clock, three o'clock. How companionable Dr. Lowell's clock seems when one is sitting up so, with no one else to talk to! Four o'clock at last; it is really growing to be quite intimate. Five o'clock. "If I were in dear Durham now, one of the roosters would be calling,"—Six o'clock. Poor Horace stirs, turns, flings his arm over. "Mother—O Huldah! is it you? How nice that is!" And he is unconscious again; but he had had sense enough to know her. What a blessed Christmas present that is, to tell that to his poor mother when she slides in at daybreak, and says, "You shall go to bed now, dear child. You see I am very fresh; and you must rest yourself, you know. Do you really say he knew you? Are you sure he knew you? Why, Huldah, what an angel of peace you are!"

So opened Huldah's Christmas morning.

Days of doubt, nights of watching. Every now and then the boy knows his mother, his father, or Huldah. Then will come this heavy stupor which is so different from sleep. At last the surgeons have determined that a piece of the bone must come away. There is the quiet gathering of the most skilful at the determined hour; there is the firm table for the little fellow to lie on; here is the ether and the sponge; and, of course, here and there, and everywhere, is Huldah. She can hold the sponge, or she can fetch and carry; she can answer at once if she is spoken to; she can wait, if it is waiting; she can act, if it is acting. At last the wretched little button, which has been pressing on our poor boy's brain, is lifted safely out. It is in Morton's hand; he smiles and nods at Huldah as she looks inquiry, and she knows he is satisfied. And does not the poor child himself, even in his unconscious sleep, draw his breath more lightly than he did before? All is well.

"Who do you say that young woman is?" says Dr. Morton to Mr. Bartlett, as he draws on his coat in the doorway after all is over. "Could we not tempt her over to the General Hospital?"

"No, I think not. I do not think we can spare her."

The boy Horace is new-born that day; a New Year's gift to his mother. So pass Huldah's holidays.

CHAPTER II

CHRISTMAS AGAIN

*F*ourteen years make of the boy whose pony has been too much for him a man equal to any prank of any pony. Fourteen years will do this, even to boys of ten. Horace Bartlett is the colonel of a cavalry regiment, stationed just now in West Virginia; and, as it happens, this twenty-four-year-old boy has an older commission than anybody in that region, and is the Post Commander at Talbot C. H., and will be, most likely, for the winter. The boy has a vein of foresight in him; a good deal of system; and, what is worth while to have by the side of system, some knack of order. So soon as he finds that he is responsible, he begins to prepare for responsibility. His staff-officers are boys too; but they are all friends, and all mean to do their best. His Surgeon-in-Charge took his degree at Washington last spring; that is encouraging. Perhaps, if he has not much experience, he has, at least, the latest advices. His head is level too; he means to do his best, such as it is; and, indeed, all hands in that knot of boy counsellors will not fail for laziness or carelessness. Their very youth makes them provident and grave.

So among a hundred other letters, as October opens, Horace writes this:—

TALBOT COURT HOUSE, VA.,
OCT. 3, 1863.

Dear Huldah,—Here we are still, as I have been explaining to father; and, as you will see by my letter to him, here we are like to stay. Thus far we are doing sufficiently well. As I have told him, if my plans had been adopted we should have been pushed rapidly forward up the valley of the Yellow Creek; Badger's corps would have been withdrawn from before Winchester; Wilcox and Steele together would have threatened Early; and then, by a rapid flank movement, we should have pounced down on Longstreet (not the great Longstreet, but little Longstreet), and compelled him to uncover Lynchburg; we could have blown up the dams and locks on the canal, made a freshet to sweep all the obstructions out of James River, and then, if they had shown half as much spirit on the Potomac, all of us would be in Richmond for our Christmas dinner. But my plans, as usual, were not asked for, far less taken. So, as I said, here we are.

Well, I have been talking with Lawrence Worster, my Surgeon-in-Charge, who is a very good fellow. His sick-list is not bad now, and he does not mean to have it bad; but he says that he is not pleased with the ways of his ward-masters; and it was his suggestion, not mine, mark you, that I should see if one or two of the Sanitary women would not come as far as this to make things decent. So, of course, I write to you. Don't you think mother could spare you to spend the winter here? It will be rough, of course; but it is all in the good cause. Perhaps you know some nice women,—well, not like you, of course; but still, disinterested and sensible, who would come too. Think of this carefully, I beg you, and talk to father and mother. Worster says we may have three hundred boys in hospital before Christmas. If Jubal Early should come this way, I don't know how many more. Talk with mother and father.

ALWAYS YOURS,

— HORACE BARTLETT

P. S. I have shown Worster what I have written; he encloses a sort of official letter which may be of use. He says, "Show this to Dr. Hayward; get them to examine you and the others, and then the government, on his order, will pass you on." I enclose this, because, if you come, it will save time.

Of course Huldah went. Grace Starr, her married sister, went with her, and Mrs. Philbrick, and Anna Thwart. That was the way they happened to be all together in the Methodist Church that had been, of Talbot Court House, as Christmas holidays drew near, of the year of grace, 1863.

She and her friends had been there quite long enough to be wonted to the strangeness of December in the open air. On her little table in front of the desk of the church were three or four buttercups in bloom, which she had gathered in an afternoon walk, with three or four heads of hawksweed. "The beginning of one year," Huldah said, "with the end of the other." Nay, there was even a stray rose which Dr. Sprigg had found in a farmer's garden. Huldah came out from the vestry, where her own bed was, in the gray of the morning, changed the water for the poor little flowers, sat a moment at the table to look at last night's memoranda, and then beckoned to the ward-master, and asked him, in a whisper, what was the movement she had heard in the night,—"Another alarm from Early?"

"No, Miss; not an alarm. I saw the Colonel's orderly as he passed. He stopped here for Dr. Fenno's case. There had come down an express from General Mitchell, and the men were called without the bugle, each man separately; not a horse was to neigh, if they could help it. And really, Miss, they were off in twenty minutes."

"Off, who are off?"

"The whole post, Miss, except the relief for to-day. There are not fifty men in the village besides us here. The orderly thought they were to go down to Braxton's; but he did not know."

Here was news indeed! news so exciting that Huldah went back at once, and called the other women; and then all of them together began on that wretched business of waiting. They had never yet known what it was to wait for a real battle. They had had their beds filled with this and that patient from one or another post, and had some gun-shot wounds of old standing among the rest; but this was their first battle if it were a battle. So the covers were taken off that long line of beds, down on the west aisle, and from those under the singers' seat; and the sheets and pillow-cases were brought out from the linen room, and aired, and put on. Our biggest kettles are filled up with strong soup; and we have our milk-punch, and our beef-tea all in readiness; and everybody we can command is on hand to help lift patients and distribute food. But there is only too much time. Will there never be any news? Anna Thwart and Doctor Sprigg have walked down to the bend of the hill, to see if any messenger is coming. As for the other women, they sit at their table; they look at their watches; they walk down to the door; they come back to the table. I notice they have all put on fresh aprons, for the sake of doing something more in getting ready.

Here is Anna Thwart. "They are coming! they are coming! somebody is coming. A mounted man is crossing the flat, coming towards us; and the doctor told me to come back and tell." Five minutes more, ten minutes more, an eternity more, and then, rat-tat-tat, rat-tat-tat, the mounted man is here. "Wagons right behind. We bagged every man of them at Wyatt's. Got there before daylight. Colonel White's men from the Yellows came up just at the same time, and we pitched in before they knew it,—three or four regiments, thirteen hundred men, and all their guns."

"And with no fighting?"

"Oh, yes! fighting of course. The colonel has got a train of wagons down here with the men that are hurt. That's why I am here. Here is his note." Thus does the mounted man discharge his errand backward.

Dear Doctor,—We have had great success. We have surprised the whole post. The company across the brook tried hard to get away; and a good many of them, and of Sykes's men, are hit; but I cannot find that we have lost more than seven men. I have nineteen wagons here of wounded men,—some hurt pretty badly.

EVER YOURS,

—H.

So there must be more waiting. But now we know what we are waiting for; and the end will come in a finite world. Thank God, at half-past three, here they are! Tenderly, gently. "Hush, Sam! Hush, Cæsar! You talk too much." Gently, tenderly. Twenty-seven of the poor fellows, with everything the matter, from a burnt face to a heart stopping its beats for want of more blood.

"Huldah, come here. This is my old classmate, Barthow; sat next me at prayers four years. He is a major in their army, you see. His horse stumbled, and pitched him against a stone wall; and he has not spoken since. Don't tell me he is dying; but do as well for him, Huldah,"—and the handsome boy smiled,—"do as well for him as you did for me." So they carried Barthow, senseless as he was, tenderly into the church; and he became E, 27, on an iron bedstead. Not half our soup was wanted, nor our beef-tea, nor our punch. So much the better.

Then came day and night, week in and out, of army system, and womanly sensibility; that quiet, cheerful, *homish*, hospital life, in the quaint surroundings of the white-washed church; the pointed arches of the windows and the faded moreen of the pulpit telling that it is a church, in a reminder not unpleasant. Two or three weeks of hopes and fears, failures and success, bring us to Christmas eve.

It is the surgeon-in-chief, who happens to give our particular Christmas dinner,—I mean the one that interests you and me. Huldah and the other ladies had accepted his invitation. Horace Bartlett and his staff, and some of the other officers, were guests; and the doctor had given his own permit that Major Barthow might walk up to his quarters with the ladies. Huldah and he were in advance, he leaning, with many apologies, on her arm. Dr. Sprigg and Anna Thwart were far behind. The two married ladies, as needing no escort, were in the middle. Major Barthow enjoyed the emancipation, was delighted with his companion, could not say enough to make her praise the glimpses of Virginia, even if it were West Virginia.

"What a party it is, to be sure!" said he. "The doctor might call on us for our stories, as one of Dickens's chiefs would do at a Christmas feast. Let's see, we should have

THE SURGEON'S TALE;

THE GENERAL'S TALE;

for we may at least make believe that Hod's stars have come from Washington. Then we must call in that one-eyed servant of his; and we will have

THE ORDERLY'S TALE.

Your handsome friend from Wisconsin shall tell

THE GERMAN'S TALE.

I shall be encouraged to tell

THE PRISONER'S TALE.

And you"—

"And I?" said Huldah laughing, because he paused.

"You shall tell

THE SAINT'S TALE."

Barthow spoke with real feeling, which he did not care to disguise. But Huldah was not there for sentiment; and without quivering in the least, nor making other acknowledgment, she laughed as she knew she ought to do, and said, "Oh, no! that is quite too grand, the story must end with

THE SUPERINTENDENT OF SPECIAL RELIEF'S TALE.

It is a little unromantic to the sound; but that's what it is."

"I don't see," persisted the major, "if Superintendent of Special Relief means Saint in Latin, why we should not say so."

"Because we are not talking Latin," said Huldah. "Listen to me; and, before we come to dinner, I will tell you a story pretty enough for Dickens, or any of them; and it is a story not fifteen minutes old.

"Have you noticed that black-whiskered fellow, under the gallery, by the north window?—Yes, the same. He is French, enlisted, I think, in New London. I came to him just now, managed to say *étrennes* and *Noël* to him, and a few other French words, and asked if there were nothing we could do to make him more at home. Oh, no! there was nothing; madame was too good, and everybody was too good, and so on. But I persisted. I wished I knew more about Christmas in France; and I staid by. 'No, madame, nothing; there is nothing. But, since you say it,—if there were two drops of red wine,—*du vin de mon pays, madame*; but you could not here in Virginia.' Could not I? A superintendent of special relief has long arms. There was a box of claret, which was the first thing I saw in the store-room the day I took my keys. The doctor was only too glad the man had thought of it;

and you should have seen the pleasure that red glass, as full as I could pile it, gave him. The tears were running down his cheeks. Anna, there, had another Frenchman; and she sent some to him: and my man is now humming a little song about the *vin rouge* of Bourgogne. Would not Mr. Dickens make a pretty story of that for you,—'The Frenchman's Story'?"

Barthow longed to say that the great novelist would not make so pretty a story as she did. But this time he did not dare.

You are not going to hear the eight stories. Mr. Dickens was not there; nor, indeed, was I. But a jolly Christmas dinner they had; though they had not those eight stories. Quiet they were, and very, very happy. It was a strange thing,—if one could have analyzed it,—that they should have felt so much at home, and so much at ease with each other, in that queer Virginian kitchen, where the doctor and his friends of his mess had arranged the feast. It was a happy thing, that the recollections of so many other Christmas homes should come in, not sadly, but pleasantly, and should cheer, rather than shade the evening. They felt off soundings, all of them. There was, for the time, no responsibility. The strain was gone. The gentlemen were glad to be dining with ladies, I believe: the ladies, unconsciously, were probably glad to be dining with gentlemen. The officers were glad they were not on duty; and the prisoner, if glad of nothing else, was glad he was not in bed. But he was glad for many things beside. You see it was but a little post. They were far away; and they took things with the ease of a detached command.

"Shall we have any toasts?" said the doctor, when his nuts and raisins and apples at last appeared.

"Oh, no! no toasts,—nothing so stiff as that."

"Oh, yes! oh, yes!" said Grace. "I should like to know what it is to drink a toast. Something I have heard of all my life, and never saw."

"One toast, at least, then," said the doctor. "Colonel Bartlett, will you name the toast?"

"Only one toast?" said Horace; "that is a hard selection: we must vote on that."

"No, no!" said a dozen voices; and a dozen laughing assistants at the feast offered their advice.

"I might give 'The Country;' I might give 'The Cause;' I might give 'The President:' and everybody would drink," said Horace. "I might give 'Absent friends,' or 'Home, sweet home;' but then we should cry."

"Why do you not give 'The trepanned people'?" said Worster, laughing, "or 'The silver-headed gentlemen'?"

"Why don't you give 'The Staff and the Line'?" "Why don't you give 'Here's Hoping'?" "Give 'Next Christmas.'" "Give 'The Medical Department; and may they often ask us to dine!'"

"Give 'Saints and Sinners,'" said Major Barthow, after the first outcry was hushed.

"I shall give no such thing," said Horace. "We have had a lovely dinner; and we know we have; and the host, who is a good fellow, knows the first thanks are not to him. Those of us who ever had our heads knocked open, like the Major and me, do know. Fill your glasses, gentlemen; I give you 'the Special Diet Kitchen.'"

He took them all by surprise. There was a general shout; and the ladies all rose, and dropped mock courtesies.

"By Jove!" said Barthow to the Colonel, afterwards, "It was the best toast I ever drank in my life. Anyway, that little woman has saved my life. Do you say she did the same to you?"

CHAPTER III

CHRISTMAS AGAIN

So you think that when the war was over Major Barthow, then Major-General, remembered Huldah all the same, and came on and persuaded her to marry him, and that she is now sitting in her veranda, looking down on the Pamunkey River. You think that, do not you?

Well! you were never so mistaken in your life. If you want that story, you can go and buy yourself a dime novel. I would buy "The Rescued Rebel;" or, "The Noble Nurse," if I were you.

After the war was over, Huldah did make Colonel Barthow and his wife a visit once, at their plantation in Pocataligo County; but I was not there, and know nothing about it.

Here is a Christmas of hers, about which she wrote a letter; and, as it happens, it was a letter to Mrs. Barthow.

HULDAH ROOT TO AGNES BARTHOW.
VILLERS-BOCAGE, DEC. 27, 1868.

. . . Here I was, then, after this series of hopeless blunders, sole alone at the *gare* [French for station] of this little out-of-the-way town. My dear, there was never an American here since Christopher Columbus slept here when he was a boy. And here, you see, I was like to remain; for there was no possibility of the others getting back to me till to-morrow, and no good in my trying to overtake them. All I could do was just to bear it, and live on, and live through from Thursday to Monday; and, really, what was worst of all was that Friday was Christmas day.

Well, I found a funny little carriage, with a funny old man who did not understand my *patois* any better than I did his; but he understood a franc-piece. I had my guide-book, and I said *auberge*; and we came to the oddest, most outlandish, and old-fashioned establishment that ever escaped from one of Julia Nathalie woman's novels. And here I am.

And the reason, my dear Mrs. Barthow, that I take to-day to write to you, you and the Colonel will now understand. You see it was only ten o'clock when I got here; then I went to walk, many *enfans terribles* following respectfully; then I came home, and ate the funny refection; then I got a nap; then I went to walk again, and made a little sketch in the churchyard: and this time, one of the children brought up her mother, a funny Norman woman, in a delicious costume,—I have a sketch of another just like her,—and she dropped a courtesy, and in a very mild *patois* said she hoped the children did not trouble madame. And I said, "Oh, no!" and found a sugar-plum for the child and showed my sketch to the woman; and she said she supposed madame was *Anglaise*.

I said I was not *Anglaise*,—and here the story begins; for I said I was *Americaine*. And, do you know, her face lighted up as if I had said I was St. Gulda, or St. Hilda, or any of their Northmen Saints.

"Americaine! est-il possible? Jeannette, Gertrude, faites vos révérences. Madame est Americaine."

And, sure enough, they all dropped preternatural courtesies. And then the most eager enthusiasm; how fond they all were of *les Americaines*, but how no *Americaines* had ever come before! And was madame at the Three Cygnets? And might she and her son and her husband call to see madame at the Three Cygnets? And might she bring a little *étrenne* to madame? And I know not what beside.

I was very glad the national reputation had gone so far. I really wished I were Charles Sumner (pardon me, dear Agnes), that I might properly receive the delegation. But I said, "Oh, certainly!" and, as it grew dark, with my admiring *cortége* whispering now to the street full of admirers that madame was *Americaine*, I returned to the Three Cygnets.

And in the evening they all came. Really, you should see the pretty basket they brought for an *étrenne*. I could not guess then where they got such exquisite flowers; these lovely stephanotis blossoms, a perfect wealth of roses, and all arranged with charming taste in a quaint country basket, such as exists nowhere but in this particular section of this quaint old Normandy. In came the husband, dressed up, and frightened, but thoroughly good in his look. In came my friend; and then two sons and two wives, and three or four children: and, my dear Agnes, one of the sons, I knew him in an instant, was a man we had at Talbot Court House when your husband was there. I think the Colonel will remember him,—a black-whiskered man, who used to sing a little song about *le vin rouge* of Bourgogne.

He did not remember me; that I saw in a moment. It was all so different, you know. In the hospital, I had on my cap and apron, and here,—well, it was another thing. My hostess knew that they were coming, and had me in her largest room, and I succeeded in making them all sit down; and I received my formal welcome; and I thanked in my most Parisian French; and then the conversation hung fire. But I took my turn now, and turned round to poor Louis.

"You served in America, did you not?" said I.

"Ah, yes, madame! I did not know my mother had told you."

No more did she, indeed; and she looked astonished. But I persevered,—

"You seem strong and well."

"Ah, yes, madame!"

"How long since you returned?"

"As soon as there was peace, madame. We were mustered out in June, madame."

"And does your arm never trouble you?"

"Oh, never, madame! I did not know my mother had told you."

New astonishment on the part of the mother.

"You never had another piece of bone come out?"

"Oh, no, madame! how did madame know? I did not know my mother had told you!"

And by this time I could not help saying, "You Normans care more for Christmas than we Americans; is it not so, my brave?"

And this he would not stand; and he said stoutly, "Ah, no, madame! no, no, *jamais!*" and began an eager defence of the religious enthusiasm of the Americans, and their goodness to all people who were good, if people would only be good. But still he had not the least dream who I was. And I said,—

"Do the Normans ever drink Burgundy?" and to my old hostess, "Madame, could you bring us a flask *du vin rouge de Bourgogne?*" and then I hummed his little chanson, I am sure

Colonel Barthow will remember it,—"*Deux—gouttes—du vin rouge du Bourgogne.*"

My dear Mrs. Barthow, he sprang from his chair, and fell on his knees, and kissed my hands, before I could stop him. And when his mother and father, and all the rest, found that I was the particular *sœur de la charité* who had had the care of dear Louis when he was hurt, and that it was I he had told of that very day,—for the thousandth time, I believe,—who gave him that glass of claret, and cheered up his Christmas, I verily believe they would have taken me to the church to worship me. They were not satisfied,—the women with kissing me, or the men with shaking hands with each other,—the whole *auberge* had to be called in; and poor I was famous. I need not say I cried my eyes out; and when, at ten o'clock, they let me go to bed, I was worn out with crying, and laughing, and talking, and listening; and I believe they were as much upset as I.

Now that is just the beginning; and yet I see I must stop. But, for forty-eight hours, I have been simply a queen. I can hardly put my foot to the ground. Christmas morning, these dear Thibault people came again; and then the *curé* came; and then some nice Madame Perrons came, and I went to mass with them; and, after mass, their brother's carriage came; and they would take no refusals; but with many apologies to my sweet old hostess, at the Three Cygnets, I was fain to come up to M. Firmin's lovely *château* here, and make myself at home till my friends shall arrive. It seems the poor Thibaults had come here to beg the flowers for the *étrenne*. It is really the most beautiful country residence I have seen in France; and they live on the most patriarchal footing with all the people round them. I am sure I ought to speak kindly of them. It is the most fascinating hospitality. So here am I, waiting, with my little *sac de nuit* to make me *aspettabile*; and here I ate my Christmas dinner. Tell the Colonel that here is "The Traveller's Tale;" and that is why the letter is so long.

Most truly yours,

— Huldah Root

CHAPTER IV

ONE CHRISTMAS MORE

This last Christmas party is Huldah's own. It is hers, at least, as much as it is any one's. There are five of them, nay, six, with equal right to precedence in the John o' Groat's house, where she has settled down. It is one of those comfortable houses which are still left three miles out from the old State House in Boston. It is not all on one floor; that would be, perhaps, too much like the golden courts of heaven. There are two stories; but they are connected by a central flight of stairs of easy tread (designed by Charles Cummings); so easy, and so stately withal, that, as you pass over them, you always bless the builder, and hardly know that you go up or down. Five large rooms on each floor give ample room for the five heads of the house, if, indeed, there be not six, as I said before.

Into this Saints' Rest, there have drifted together, by the eternal law of attraction,—Huldah, and Ellen Philbrick (who was with her in Virginia, and in France, and has been, indeed, but little separated from her, except on duty, for twenty years), and with them three other friends. These women,—well, I cannot introduce them to you without writing three stories of true romance, one for each. This quiet, strong, meditative, helpful saint, who is coming into the parlor now, is Helen Touro. She was left alone with her baby when "The Empire State" went down; and her husband was never heard of more. The love of that baby warmed her to the love of all others; and, when I first knew her, she was ruling over a home of babies, whose own mothers or fathers were not,— always with a heart big enough to say there was room for one more waif in that sanctuary. That older woman, who is writing at the Davenport in the corner, lightened the cares and smoothed the daily life of General Schuyler in all the last years of his life, when he was in the Cabinet, in Brazil, and in Louisiana. His wife was long ill, and then died. His children needed all a woman's care; and this woman stepped to the front, cared for them, cared for all his house- hold, cared for him: and I dare not say how much is due to her of that which you and I say daily we owe to him. Miss Peters, I see you know. She served in another regiment; was at the head of the sweetest, noblest, purest school that ever trained, in five and twenty years, five hundred girls to be the queens in five hundred happy and strong families. All of these five,—our Huldah and Mrs. Philbrick too, you have seen before,—all of them have been in "the service;" all of them have known that perfect service is perfect freedom. I think they know that perfect service is the highest honor. They have together taken this house, as they say, for the shelter and home of their old age. But Huldah, as she plays with your Harry there, does not look to me as if she were superannuated yet.

"But you said there were six in all."

Did I? I suppose there are. "Mrs. Philbrick, are there five captains in your establishment, or six?"

"My dear Mr. Hale, why do you ask me? You know there are five captains and one general. We have persuaded Seth Corbet to make his home here,—yes, the same who went round the world with Mrs. Cradock. Since her death, he has come home to Boston; and he reports to us, and makes his head-quarters here. He sees that we are all right every morning; and then he goes his rounds to see every grandchild of old Mr. Cradock, and to make sure that every son and daughter of that house is 'all right.' Sometimes he is away over night. This is when somebody in the whole circle of all their friends is more sick than usual, and needs a man nurse. That old man was employed by old Mr. Cradock, in 1816, when he first went to housekeeping. He has had all the sons and all the daughters of that house in his arms; and now that the youngest of them is five and twenty, and the oldest fifty, I suppose he is not satisfied any day until he has seen that they and theirs, in their respective homes, are well. He thinks we here are babies; but he takes care of us all the more courteously."

"Will he dine with you to-day?"

"I am afraid not; but we shall see him at the Christmas-tree after dinner. There is to be a tree."

You see, this house was dedicated to the Apotheosis of Noble Ministry. Over the mantel-piece hung Raphael Morghen's large print of "The Lavatio," Caracci's picture of "The Washing of the Feet,"—the only copy I ever saw. We asked Huldah about it.

"Oh, that was a present from Mr. Burchstadt, a rich manufacturer in Würtemberg, to Ellen. She stumbled into one of those villages when everybody was sick and dying of typhus, and tended and watched and saved, one whole summer long, as Mrs. Ware did at Osmotherly. And this Mr. Burchstadt wanted to do something, and he sent her this in acknowledgment."

On the other side was Kaulbach's own study of Elizabeth of Hungary, dropping her apron full of roses.

> "Oh! what a sight the apron discloses;
> The viands are changed to real roses!"

When I asked Huldah where that came from, she blushed, and said, "Oh, that was a present to me!" and led us to Steinler's exquisite "Good Shepherd," in a larger and finer print than I had ever seen. Six or eight gentlemen in New York, who, when they were dirty babies from the gutter, had been in Helen Touro's hands, had sent her a portfolio of beautiful prints, each with this same idea, of seeking what was lost. This one she had chosen for the sitting-room.

And, on the fourth side, was that dashing group of Horace Vernet's, "Gideon crossing Jordan," with the motto wrought into the frame, "Faint, yet pursuing." These four pictures are all presents to the "girls," as I find I still call them; and, on the easel, Miss Peters had put her copy of "The Tribute Money." There were other pictures in the room; but these five unconsciously told its story.

The five "girls" were always all together at Christmas; but, in practice, each of them lived here only two-fifths of her time. "We make that a rule," said Ellen laughing. "If anybody comes for anybody when there are only two here, those two are engaged to each other; and we stay. Not but what they can come and stay here if we cannot go to them." In practice, if any of us in the immense circles which these saints had befriended were in a scrape,—as, if a mother was called away from home, and there were some children left, or if scarlet fever got into a house, or if the children had nobody to go to Mt. Desert with them, or if the new house were to be set in order, and nobody knew how,—in any of the trials of well-ordered families, why, we rode over to the Saints' Rest to see if we could not induce one of the five to come and put things through. So that, in practice, there were seldom more than two on the spot there.

But we do not get to the Christmas dinner. There were covers for four and twenty; and all the children besides were in a room upstairs, presided over by Maria Munro, who was in her element there. Then our party of twenty-four included men and women of a thousand romances, who had learned and had shown the nobility of service. One or two of us were invited as novices, in the hope perhaps that we might learn.

Scarcely was the soup served when the door-bell rang. Nothing else ever made Huldah look nervous. Bartlett, who was there, said in an aside to me, that he had seen her more calm when there was volley firing within hearing of her store-room. Then it rang again. Helen Touro talked more vehemently; and Mrs. Bartlett at her end, started a great laugh. But, when it rang the third time, something had to be said; and Huldah asked one of the girls, who was waiting, if there were no one attending at the door.

"Yes 'm, Mr. Corbet."

But the bell rang a fourth time, and a fifth.

"Isabel, you can go to the door. Mr. Corbet must have stepped out."

So Isabel went out, but returned with a face as broad as a soup-plate. "Mr. Corbet is there, ma'am."

Sixth door-bell peal,—seventh, and eighth.

"Mary, I think you had better see if Mr. Corbet has gone away."

Mary returns, face one broad grin.

"No, ma'am, Mr. Corbet is there."

Heavy steps in the red parlor. Side door-bell—a little gong, begins to ring. Front bell rings ninth time, tenth, and eleventh.

Saint John, as we call him, had seen that something was amiss, and had kindly pitched in with a dissertation on the passage of the Red-River Dam, in which the gravy-boats were steamships, and the cranberry was General Banks, and the aids were spoons. But, when both door-bells rang together, and there were more steps in the hall, Huldah said, "If you will excuse me," and rose from the table.

"No, no, we will not excuse you," cried Clara Hastings. "Nobody will excuse you. This is the one day of the year when you are not to work. Let me go." So Clara went out. And after Clara went out, the door-bells rang no more. I think she cut the bell-wires. She soon came back, and said a man was inquiring his way to the "Smells;" and they directed him to "Wait's Mills," which she hoped would do. And so Huldah's and Grace's stupendous housekeeping went on in its solid order, reminding one of those well-proportioned Worcester teas which are, perhaps, the crown and glory of the New England science in this matter. I ventured to ask Sam Root, who sat by me, if the Marlborough were not equal to his mother's.

And we sat long; and we laughed loud. We talked war and poetry and genealogy. We rallied Helen Touro about her housekeeping; and Dr. Worster pretended to give a list of Surgeons and Majors and Major-Generals who had made love to Huldah. By and by, when the grapes and the bonbons came, the sixteen children were led in by Maria Munro, who had, till now, kept them at games of string and hunt the slipper. And, at last, Seth Corbet flung open the door into the red parlor to announce "The Tree."

Sure enough, there was the tree, as the five saints had prepared it for the invited children,—glorious in gold, and white with wreaths of snow-flakes, and blazing with candles. Sam Root kissed Grace, and said, "O Grace! do you remember?" But the tree itself did not surprise the children as much as the five tables at the right and the left, behind and before, amazed the Sainted Five, who were indeed the children now. A box of the *vin rouge de Bourgogne*, from Louis, was the first thing my eye lighted on, and above it a little banner read, "Huldah's table." And then I saw that there were these five tables, heaped with the Christmas offerings to the five saints. It proved that everybody, the world over, had heard that they had settled down. Everybody in the four hemispheres,—if there be four,—who had remembered the unselfish service of these five, had thought this a fit time for commemorating such unselfish love, were it only by such a present as a lump of coal. Almost everybody, I think, had made Seth Corbet a confidant; and so, while the five saints were planning their pretty tree for the sixteen children, the North and the South, and the East and the West, were sending myrrh and frankincense and gold to them. The pictures were hung with Southern moss from Barthow. Boys, who were now men, had sent coral from India, pearl from Ceylon, and would have been glad to send ice from Greenland, had Christmas come in midsummer; there were diamonds from Brazil, and silver from Nevada, from those who lived there; there were books, in the choicest binding, in memory of copies of the same word, worn by travel, or dabbled in blood; there were pictures, either by the hand of near friendship, or by the master hand of genius, which brought back the memories, perhaps, of some old adventure in "The Service,"—perhaps, as the Kaulbach did, of one of those histories which makes all service sacred. In five and twenty years of life, these women had so surrounded themselves, without knowing it or thinking of it, with loyal, yes, adoring friends, that the accident of their finding a fixed home had called in all at once this wealth of acknowledgment from those whom they might have forgotten, but who would never forget them. And, by the accident of our coming together, we saw, in these heaps on heaps of offerings of love, some faint record of the lives they had enlivened, the wounds they had stanched, the tears they had wiped away, and the homes they had cheered. For themselves, the five saints—as I have called them—were laughing and crying together, quite upset in the surprise. For ourselves, there was not one of us who, in this little visible display of the range of years of service, did not take in something more of the meaning of,—

"He who will be chief among you, let him be your servant."

The surprise, the excitement, the laughter, and the tears found vent in the children's eagerness to be led to their tree; and, in three minutes, Ellen was opening boxes, and Huldah pulling fire-crackers, as if they had not been thrown off their balance. But, when each boy and girl had two arms full, and the fir balsam sent down from New Durham was nearly bare, Edgar Bartlett pointed to the top bough, where was a brilliant not noticed before. No one had noticed it,—not Seth himself,—who had most of the other secrets of that house in his possession. I am sure that no man, woman, or child knew how the thing came there: but Seth lifted the little discoverer high in air, and he brought it down triumphant. It was a parcel made up in shining silvered paper. Seth cut the strings.

It contained twelve Maltese crosses of gold, with as many jewels, one in the heart of each,—I think the blazing twelve of the Revelations. They were displayed on ribbons of blue and white, six of which bore Huldah's, Helen's, Ellen Philbrick's, Hannah's, Miss Peters's, and Seth Corbet's names. The other six had no names; but on the gold of these was marked,—"From Huldah, to ——" "From Helen, to ——" and so on, as if these were decorations which they were to pass along. The saints themselves were the last to understand the decorations; but the rest of us caught the idea, and pinned them on their breasts. As we did so, the ribbons unfolded, and displayed the motto of the order:—

"Henceforth I call you not servants, I have called you friends."

It was at that Christmas that the "Order of Loving Service" was born.

The Two Princes

A STORY FOR CHILDREN

CHAPTER I

There was a King of Hungary whose name was Adelbert.

When he lived at home, which was not often, it was in a castle of many towers and many halls and many stairways, in the city of Buda, by the side of the river Donau.

He had four daughters, and only one son, who was to be the King after him, whose name was Ladislaus. But it was the custom of those times, as boys and girls grew up, to send them for their training to some distance from their home, even for many months at a time, to try a little experiment on them, and see how they fared; and so, at the time I tell you of, there was staying in the castle of Buda the Prince Bela, who was the son of the King of Bohemia; and he and the boy Ladislaus studied their lessons together, and flew their kites, and hunted for otters, and rode with the falconers together.

One day as they were studying with the tutor, who was a priest named Stephen, he gave to them a book of fables, and each read a fable.

Ladislaus read the fable of the

Sky-Lark

The sky-lark sat on the topmost bough of the savy-tree, and was waked by the first ray of the sun. Then the sky-lark flew and flew up and up to the topmost arch of the sky, and sang the hymn of the morning.

But a frog, who was croaking in the cranberry marsh, said, "Why do you take such pains and fly so high? the sun shines here, and I can sing here."

And the bird said, "God has made me to fly. God has made me to see. I will fly as high as He will lift me, and sing so loud that all shall hear me."

And when the little Prince Ladislaus had read the fable, he cried out, "The sky-lark is the bird for me, and I will paint his picture on my shield after school this morning."

Then the Prince Bela read the next fable,—the fable of the

Water-Rat

A good beaver found one day a little water-rat almost dead. His father and mother had been swept away by a freshet, and the little rat was almost starved. But the kind beaver gave him of her own milk, and brought him up in her own lodge with her children, and he got well, and could eat, and swim, and dive with the best of them.

But one day there was a great alarm, that the beavers' dam was giving way before the water. "Come one, come all," said the grandfather of the beavers, "come to the rescue." So they all started, carrying sticks and bark with them, the water-rat and all. But as they swam under an old oak-tree's root, the water-rat stopped in the darkness, and then he quietly turned round and went back to the hut. "It will be hard work," said he "and there are enough of them." There were enough of them. They mended the dam by working all night and by working all day. But, as they came back, a great wave of the freshet came pouring over the dam and, though the dam stood firm, the beavers were swept away,—away and away, down the river into the sea, and they died there.

And the water-rat lived in their grand house by himself, and had all their stores of black-birch bark and willow bark and sweet poplar bark for his own.

"That was a clever rat," said the Prince Bela. "I will paint the rat on my shield, when school is done." And the priest Stephen was very sad when he said so; and the Prince Ladislaus was surprised.

So they went to the play-room and painted their shields. The shields were made of the bark of hemlock-trees. Ladislaus chipped off the rough bark till the shield was white, and made on the place the best sky-lark he could paint there. And Bela watched him, and chipped off the rough bark from his shield, and said, "You paint so well, now paint my water-rat for me." "No," said Ladislaus, though he was very good-natured, "I cannot paint it well. You must paint it yourself." And Bela did so.

CHAPTER II

So the boys both grew up, and one became King of Hungary, and one was the King of the Bohemians. And King Ladislaus carried on his banner the picture of a sky-lark; and the ladies of the land embroidered sky-larks for the scarfs and for the pennons of the soldiers, and for the motto of the banner were the Latin words "Propior Deo," which mean "Nearer to God." And King Bela carried the water-rat for his cognizance; and the ladies of his land embroidered water-rats for the soldiers; and his motto was "Enough."

And in these times a holy man from Palestine came through all the world; and he told how the pilgrims to the tomb of Christ were beaten and starved by the Saracens, and how many of them were dying in dungeons. And he begged the princes and the lords and ladies, for the love of God and the love of Christ, that they would come and rescue these poor people, and secure the pilgrims in all coming time. And King Ladislaus said to his people, "We will do the best we can, and serve God as He shows us how!" And the people said, "We will do the best we can, and save the people of Christ from the infidel!" And they all came together to the place of arms; and the King chose a hundred of the bravest and healthiest of the young men, all of whom told the truth, and no one of whom was afraid to die, and they marched with him to the land of Christ; and as they marched they sang, "Propior Deo,"—"Nearer to Thee."

And Peter the Hermit went to Bohemia, and told the story of the cruel Saracens and the sufferings of the pilgrims to King Bela and his people. And the King said, "Is it far away?" And the Hermit said, "Far, far away." And the King said, "Ah, well,—they must get out as they got in. We will take care of Bohemia." So the Hermit went on to Saxony, to tell his story.

And King Ladislaus and his hundred true young men rode and rode day by day, and came to the Mount of Olives just in time to be at the side of the great King Godfrey, when he broke the Paynim's walls, and dashed into the city of Jerusalem. And King Ladislaus and his men rode together along the Way of Tears, where Christ bore the cross-beam upon his shoulder, and he sat on the stone where the cross had been reared, and he read the gospel through again; and there he prayed his God that he might always bear his cross bravely, and that, like the Lord Jesus, he might never be afraid to die.

CHAPTER III

*A*nd when they had all come home to Hungary, their time hung very heavy on their hands. And the young men said to the King, "Lead us to war against the Finns, or lead us to war against the Russ."

But the King said, "No! if they spare our people, we spare their people. Let us have peace." And he called the young men who had fought with him, and he said, "The time hangs heavy with us; let us build a temple here to the living God, and to the honor of his Son. We will carve on its walls the story we have seen, and while we build we will remember Zion and the Way of Tears."

And the young men said, "We are not used to building."

"Nor am I," said the King; "but let us build, and build as best we can, and give to God the best we have and the best we know."

So they dug the deep trenches for the foundations, and they sent north and south, and east and west for the wisest builders who loved the Lord Christ; and the builders came, and the carvers came, and the young men learned to use the chisel and the hammer; and the great Cathedral grew year by year, as a pine-tree in the forest grows above the birches and the yew-trees on the ground.

And once King Bela came to visit his kinsman, and they rode out to see the builders. And King Ladislaus dismounted from his horse, and asked Bela to dismount, and gave to him a chisel and a hammer.

"No," said the King Bela, "it will hurt my hands. In my land we have workmen whom we pay to do these things. But I like to see you work."

So he sat upon his horse till dinner-time, and he went home.

And year by year the Cathedral grew. And a thousand pinnacles were built upon the towers and on the roof and along the walls; and on each pinnacle there fluttered a golden sky-lark. And on the altar in the Cathedral was a scroll of crimson, and on the crimson scroll were letters of gold, and the letters were in the Latin language, and said "Propior Deo," and on a blue scroll underneath, in the language of the people they were translated, and it said, "Nearer to Thee."

CHAPTER IV

And another Hermit came, and he told the King that the Black Death was ravaging the cities of the East; that half the people of Constantinople were dead; that the great fair at Adrianople was closed; that the ships on the Black Sea had no sailors; and that there would be no food for the people on the lower river.

And the King said, "Is the Duke dead, whom we saw at Bucharest; is the Emperor dead, who met me at Constantinople?"

"No, your Grace," said the Hermit, "it pleases the Lord that in the Black Death only those die who live in hovels and in towns. The Lord has spared those who live in castles and in palaces."

"Then," said King Ladislaus, "I will live as my people live, and I will die as my people die. The Lord Jesus had no pillow for his head, and no house for his lodging; and as the least of his brethren fares so will I fare, and as I fare so shall they."

So the King and the hundred braves pitched their tents on the high land above the old town, around the new Cathedral, and the Queen and the ladies of the court went with them. And day by day the King and the Queen and the hundred braves and their hundred ladies went up and down the filthy wynds and courts of the city, and they said to the poor people there, "Come, live as we live, and die as we die."

And the people left the holes of pestilence and came and lived in the open air of God.

And when the people saw that the King fared as they fared, the people said, "We also will seek God as the King seeks Him, and will serve Him as he serves Him."

And day by day they found others who had no homes fit for Christian men, and brought them upon the high land and built all together their tents and booths and tabernacles, open to the sun and light, and to the smile and kiss and blessing of the fresh air of God. And there grew a new and beautiful city there.

And so it was, that when the Black Death passed from the East to the West, the Angel of Death left the city of Buda on one side, and the people never saw the pestilence with their eyes. The Angel of Death passed by them, and rested upon the cities of Bohemia.

CHAPTER V

And King Ladislaus grew old. His helmet seemed to him more heavy. His sleep seemed to him more coy. But he had little care, for he had a loving wife, and he had healthy, noble sons and daughters, who loved God, and who told the truth, and who were not afraid to die.

But one day, in his happy prosperity, there came to him a messenger running, who said in the Council, "Your Grace, the Red Russians have crossed the Red River of the north, and they are marching with their wives and their children with their men of arms in front, and their wagons behind, and they say they will find a land nearer the sun, and to this land are they coming."

And the old King smiled; and he said to those that were left of the hundred brave men who took the cross with him, "Now we will see if our boys could have fought at Godfrey's side. For us it matters little. One way or another way we shall come nearer to God."

And the armorers mended the old armor, and the young men girded on swords which had never been tried in fight, and the pennons that they bore were embroidered by their sweethearts and sisters as in the old days of the Crusades, and with the same device of a sky-lark in mid-heaven, and the motto, "Nearer, my God, to Thee."

And there came from the great Cathedral the wise men who had come from all the lands. They found the King, and they said to him, "Your Grace, we know how to build the new defences for the land, and we will guard the river ways, that the barbarians shall never enter them."

And when the people knew that the Red Russians were on the way, they met in the square and marched to the palace, and Robert the Smith mounted the steps of the palace and called the King. And he said, "The people are here to bid the King be of good heart. The people bid me say that they will die for their King and for his land."

And the King took from his wife's neck the blue ribbon that she wore, with a golden sky-lark on it, and bound it round the blacksmith's arm, and he said, "If I die, it is nothing; if I live, it is nothing; that is in God's hand. But whether we live or die, let us draw as near Him as we may."

And the Blacksmith Robert turned to the people, and with his loud voice, told what the King had said.

And the people answered in the shout which the Hungarians shout to this day, "Let us die for our king! Let us die for our king!"

And the King called the Queen hastily, and they and their children led the host to the great Cathedral.

And the old priest Stephen, who was ninety years old, stood at the altar, and he read the gospel where it says, "Fear not, little flock, it is your Father's good pleasure to give you the kingdom."

And he read the other gospel where the Lord says, "And I, if I be lifted up, will draw all men unto me." And he read the epistle where it says, "No man liveth to himself, and no man dieth to himself." And he chanted the psalm, "The Lord is my rock, my fortress, and my deliverer."

And fifty thousand men, with one heart and one voice, joined with him. And the King joined, and the Queen to sing, "The Lord is my rock, my fortress, and my deliverer."

And they marched from the Cathedral, singing in the language of the country, "Propior Deo," which is to say in our tongue, "Nearer, my God, to Thee."

And the aged braves who had fought with Godfrey, and the younger men who had learned of arms in the University, went among the people and divided them into companies for the war. And Robert the Blacksmith, and all the guild of the blacksmiths, and of the braziers, and of the coppersmiths, and of the whitesmiths, even the goldsmiths, and the silversmiths, made weapons for the war; and the masons and the carpenters, and the ditchers and delvers marched out with the cathedral builders to the narrow passes of the river, and built new the fortresses.

And the Lady Constance and her daughters, and every lady in the land, went to the churches and the convents, and threw them wide open. And in the kitchens they baked bread for the soldiers; and in the churches they spread couches for the sick or for the wounded.

And when the Red Russians came in their host, there was not a man, or woman, or child in all Hungary but was in the place to which God had called him, and was doing his best in his place for his God, for the Church of Christ, and for his brothers and sisters of the land.

And the host of the Red Russians was turned aside, as at the street corner you have seen the dirty water of a gutter turned aside by the curbstone. They fought one battle against the Hungarian host, and were driven as the blackbirds are driven by the falcons. And they gathered themselves and swept westward; and came down upon the passes to Bohemia.

And there were no fortresses at the entrance to Bohemia; for King Bela had no learned men who loved him. And there was no army in the plains of Bohemia; for his people had been swept away in the pestilence. And there were no brave men who had fought with Godfrey, and knew the art of arms, for in those old days the King had said, "It is far away; and we have 'enough' in Bohemia."

So the Red Russians, who call themselves the Szechs, took his land from him; and they live there till this day. And the King, without a battle, fled from the back-door of his palace, in the disguise of a charcoal-man; and he left his queen and his daughters to be cinder-girls in the service of the Chief of the Red Russians.

And the false charcoal-man walked by day, and walked by night, till he found refuge in the castle of the King Ladislaus; and he met him in the old school-room where they read the fables together. And he remembered how the water-rat came to the home of the beavers.

And he said to King Ladislaus,—

"Ah, me! do you remember when we were boys together? Do you remember the fable of the Sky-lark, and the fable of the Water-rat?"

"I remember both," said the King. And he was silent.

"God has been very kind to you," said the beggar; "and He has been very hard to me."

And the King said nothing.

But the old priest Stephen, said,—

"God is always kind. But God will not give us other fruit than we sow seed for. The King here has tried to serve God as he knew how; with one single eye he has looked on the world of God, and he has made the best choice he knew. And God has given him what he thought not of: brave men for his knights; wise men for his council; a free and loving people for his army. And you have not looked with a single eye; your eye was darkened. You saw only what served yourself. And you said, 'This is enough;' and you had no brave men for your knights; no wise men for your council; no people for your army. You chose to look down, and to take a selfish brute for your adviser. And he has led you so far. We choose to look up; to draw nearer God; and where He leads we follow."

Then King Ladislaus ordered that in the old school-room a bed should be spread for Bela; and that every day his breakfast and his dinner and his supper should be served to him; and he lived there till he died.

The Story of Oello

O nce upon a time there was a young girl, who had the pretty name of Oello. I say, once upon a time, because I do not know when the time was,—nor do I know what the place was,—though my story, in the main, is a true story. I do not mean that I sat by and saw Oello when she wove and when she spun. But I know she did weave and did spin. I do not mean that I heard her speak the word I tell of; for it was many, many hundred years ago. But I do know that she must have said some such words; for I know many of the things which she did, and much of what kind of girl she was.

She grew up like other girls in her country. She did not know how to read. None of them knew how to read. But she knew how to braid straw, and to make fish-nets and to catch fish. She did not know how to spell. Indeed, in that country they had no letters. But she knew how to split open the fish she had caught, how to clean them, how to broil them on the coals, and how to eat them neatly. She had never studied the "analysis of her language." But she knew how to use it like a lady; that is, prettily, simply, without pretence, and always truly. She could sing her baby brother to sleep. She could tell stories to her sisters all day long. And she and they were not afraid when evening came, or when they were in any trouble, to say a prayer aloud to the good God. So they got along, although they could not analyze their language. She knew no geography. She could count her fingers, and the stars in the Southern Cross. She had never seen Orion, or the stars in the Great Bear, or the Pole-Star.

Oello was very young when she married a young kinsman, with whom she had grown up since they were babies. Nobody knows much about him. But he loved her and she loved him. And when morning came they were not afraid to pray to God together,—and when night came she asked her husband to forgive her if she had troubled him, and he asked her to forgive him,—so that their worries and trials never lasted out the day. And they lived a very happy life, till they were very old and died.

There is a bad gap in the beginning of their history. I do not know how it happened. But the first I knew of them, they had left their old home and were wandering alone on foot toward the South. Sometimes I have thought a great earthquake had wrecked their old happy home. Sometimes I have thought there was some horrid pestilence, or fire. No matter what happened, something happened,—so that Oello and her husband, of a hot, very hot day, were alone under a forest of laurels mixed with palms, with bright flowering orchids on them, looking like a hundred butterflies; ferns, half as high as the church is, tossing over them; nettles as large as trees, and tangled vines, threading through the whole. They were tired, oh, how tired!

hungry, oh, how hungry! and hot and foot-sore.

"I wish so we were out of this hole," said he to her, "and yet I am afraid of the people we shall find when we come down to the lake side."

"I do not know," said Oello, "why they should want to hurt us."

"I do not know why they should want to," said he, "but I am afraid they will hurt us."

"But we do not want to hurt them," said she. "For my part, all I want is a shelter to live under; and I will help them take care of their children, and

'I will spin their flax,
And weave their thread,
And pound their corn,
And bake their bread.'"

"How will you tell them that you will do this?" said he.

"I will do it," said Oello, "and that will be better than telling them."

"But do not you just wish," said he, "that you could speak five little words of their language, to say to them that we come as friends, and not as enemies?"

Oello laughed very heartily. "Enemies," said she, "terrible enemies, who have two sticks for their weapons, two old bags for their stores, and cotton clothes for their armor. I do not believe more than half the army will turn out against us." So Oello pulled out the potatoes from the ashes, and found they were baked; she took a little salt from her haversack or scrip, and told her husband that dinner would be ready, if he would only bring some water. He pretended to groan, but went, and came in a few minutes with two gourds full, and they made a very merry meal.

The same evening they came cautiously down on the beautiful meadow land which surrounded the lake they had seen. It is one of the most beautiful countries in the world. It was an hour before sunset,—the hour, I suppose, when all countries are most beautiful. Oello and her husband came joyfully down the hill, through a little track the llamas had made toward the water, wondering at the growth of the wild grasses, and, indeed, the freshness of all the green; when they were startled by meeting a horde of the poor, naked, half-starved Indians, who were just as much alarmed to meet with them.

I do not think that the most stupid of them could have supposed Oello an enemy, nor her husband. For they stepped cheerfully down the path, waving boughs of fresh cinchona as tokens of peace, and looking kindly and pleasantly on the poor Indians, as I believe nobody had looked on them before. There were fifty of the savages, but it was true that they were as much afraid of the two young Northerners as if they had been an army. They saw them coming down the hill, with the western sun behind them, and one of the women cried out, "They are children of the sun, they are children of the sun!" and Oello and her husband looked so as if they had come from a better world that all the other savages believed it.

But the two young people came down so kindly and quickly, that the Indian women could not well run away. And when Oello caught one of the little babies up, and tossed it in her arms, and fondled it, and made it laugh, the little girl's mother laughed too. And when they had all once laughed together, peace was made among them all, and Oello saw where the Indian women had been lying, and what their poor little shelters were, and she led the way there, and sat down on a log that had fallen there, and called the children round her, and began teaching them a funny game with a bit of crimson cord. Nothing pleases savage people or tame people more than attention to their children, and in less time than I have been telling this they were all good friends. The Indian women produced supper. Pretty poor supper it was. Some fresh-water clams from the lake, some snails which Oello really shuddered at, but some bananas which were very nice, and some ulloco, a root Oello had never seen before, and which she thought sickish. But she acted on her motto. "I will do the best I can," she had said all along; so she ate and drank, as if she had always been used to raw snails and to ulloco, and made the wild women laugh by trying to imitate the names of the strange food. In a few minutes after supper the sun set. There is no twilight in that country. When the sun goes down,

"Like battle target red,—
He rushes to his burning bed,
Dyes the whole wave with ruddy light,
Then sinks at once, and all is night."

The savage people showed the strangers a poor little booth to sleep in, and went away to their own lairs, with many prostrations, for they really thought them "children of the sun."

Oello and her husband laughed very heartily when they knew they were alone. Oello made him promise to go in the morning early for potatoes, and oca, and mashua, which are two other tubers like potatoes which grow there. "And we will show them," said she, "how to cook them." For they had seen by the evening feast, that the poor savage people had no knowledge of the use of fire. So, early in the morning, he went up a little way on the lake shore, and returned with strings of all these roots, and with another string of fish he had caught in a brook above. And when the savage people waked and came to Oello's hut, they found her and her husband just starting their fire,—a feat these people had never seen before.

He had cut with his copper knife a little groove in some soft palm-wood, and he had fitted in it a round piece of iron-wood, and round the iron-wood had bound a bow-string, and while Oello held the palm-wood firm, he made the iron-wood fly round and round and round, till the pith of the palm smoked, and smoked, and at last a flake of the pith caught fire, and then another and another, and Oello dropped other flakes upon these, and blew them gently, and fed them with dry leaves, till they were all in a blaze.

The savage people looked on with wonder and terror. They cried out when they saw the blaze, "They are children of the sun,—they are children of the sun!"—and ran away. Oello and her husband did not know what they said, and went on broiling the fish and baking the potatoes, and the mashua, and the oca, and the ulloco.

And when they were ready, Oello coaxed some of the children to come back, and next their mothers came and next the men. But still they said, "They are children of the sun." And when they ate of the food that had been cooked for them, they said it was the food of the immortals.

Now, in Oello's home, this work of making the fire from wood had been called menial work, and was left to servants only. But even the princes of that land were taught never to order another to do what they could not do themselves. And thus it happened that the two young travellers could do it so well. And thus it was, that, because they did what they could, the savage people honored them with such exceeding honor, and because they did the work of servants they called them gods. As it is written: "He who is greatest among you shall be your servant."

And this was much the story of that day and many days. While her husband went off with the men, taught them how he caught the fish, and how they could catch huanacos, Oello sat in the shade with the children, who were never tired of pulling at the crimson cord around her waist, and at the tassels of her head-dress. All savage children are curious about the dress of their visitors. So it was easy for Oello to persuade them to go with her and pick tufts of wild cotton, till they had quite a store of it, and then to teach them to spin it on distaffs she made for them from laurel-wood, and at last to braid it and to knit it,—till at last one night, when the men came home, Oello led out thirty of the children in quite a grand procession, dressed all of them in pretty cotton suits they had knit for themselves, instead of the filthy, greasy skins they had always worn before. This was a great triumph for Oello; but when the people would gladly have worshipped her, she only said, "I did what I could,—I did what I could,—say no more, say no more."

And as the year passed by, she and her husband taught the poor people how, if they would only plant the maize, they could have all they wanted in the winter, and if they planted the roots of the ulloco, and the oca, and the mashua, and the potato, they would have all they needed of them; how they might make long fish-ways for the fish, and pitfalls for the llama. And they learned the language of the poor people, and taught them the language to which they themselves were born. And year by year their homes grew neater and more cheerful. And year by year the children were stronger and better. And year by year the world in that part of it was more and more subdued to the will and purpose of a good God. And whenever Manco, Oello's husband, was discouraged, she always said, "We will do the best we can," and always it proved that that was all that a good God wanted them to do.

It was from the truth and steadiness of those two people, Manco and Oello, that the great nation of Peru was raised up from a horde of savages, starving in the mountains, to one of the most civilized and happy nations of their times. Unfortunately for their descendants, they did not learn the use of iron or gunpowder, so that the cruel Spaniards swept them and theirs away. But for hundreds of years they lived peacefully and happily,— growing more and more civilized with every year, because the young Oello and her husband Manco had done what they could for them.

They did not know much. But what they knew they could do. They were not, so far as we know, skilful in talking. But they were cheerful in acting.

They did not hide their light under a bushel. They made it shine on all that came around. Their duties were the humblest, only making a fire in the morning, cleaning potatoes and cooking them, spinning, braiding, twisting, and weaving. This was the best Oello could do. She did that, and in doing it she reared an empire. We can contrast her life with that of the savages around her. As we can see a drop of blood when it falls into a cup of water, we can see how that one life swayed theirs. If she had lived among her kindred, and done at home these simple things, we should never have heard her name. But none the less would she have done them. None the less, year in and year out, century in and century out, would that sweet, loving, true, unselfish life have told in God's service. And he would have known it, though you and I—who are we?—had never heard her name!

Forgotten! do not ever think that anything is forgotten!

Love is the Whole

A STORY FOR CHILDREN

This is a story about some children who were living together in a Western State, in a little house on the prairie, nearly two miles from any other. There were three boys and three girls; the oldest girl was seventeen, and her oldest brother a year younger. Their mother had died two or three years before, and now their father grew sick,—more sick and more, and died also. The children were taking the best care they could of him, wondering and watching. But no care could do much, and so he told them. He told them all that he should not live long; but that when he died he should not be far from them, and should be with their dear mother. "Remember," he said, "to love each other. Be kind to each other. Stick together, if you can. Or, if you separate, love one another as if you were together." He did not say any more then. He lay still awhile, with his eyes closed; but every now and then a sweet smile swept over his face, so that they knew he was awake. Then he roused up once more, and said, "Love is the whole, George; love is the whole,"—and so he died.

I have no idea that the children, in the midst of their grief and loneliness, took in his meaning. But afterwards they remembered it again and again, and found out why he said it to them.

Any of you would have thought it a queer little house. It was not a log cabin. They had not many logs there. But it was no larger than the log cabin which General Grant is building in the picture. There was a little entry-way at one end, and two rooms opening on the right as you went. A flight of steps went up into the loft, and in the loft the boys slept in two beds. This was all. But if they had no rooms for servants, on the other hand they had no servants for rooms. If they had no hot-water pipes, on the other hand a large kettle hung on the crane above the kitchen fire, and there was but a very short period of any day that one could not dip out hot water. They had no gas-pipes laid through the house. But they went to bed the earlier, and were the more sure to enjoy the luxury of the great morning illumination by the sun. They lost but few steps in going from room to room. They were never troubled for want of fresh air. They had no door-bell, so no guest was ever left waiting in the cold. And though they had no speaking-tubes in the house, still they found no difficulty in calling each other if Ethan were up stairs and Alice wanted him to come down.

Their father was buried, and the children were left alone. The first night after the funeral they stole to their beds as soon as they could, after the mock supper was over. The next morning George and Fanny found themselves the first to meet at the kitchen hearth. Each had tried to anticipate the other in making the morning fire. Each confessed to the other that there had been but little sleep, and that the night had seemed hopelessly long.

"But I have thought it all over," said the brave, stout boy. "Father told us to stick together as long as we can. And I know I can manage it. The children will all do their best when they understand it. And I know, though father could not believe it, I know that I can manage with the team. We will never get in debt. I shall never drink. Drink and debt, as he used to say, are the only two devils. Never you cry, darling Fanny, I know we can get along."

"George," said Fanny, "I know we can get along if you say so. I know it will be very hard upon you. There are so many things the other young men do which you will not be able to do; and so many things which they have which you might have. But none of them has a sister who loves them as I love you. And, as he said, 'Love is the whole.'"

I suppose those words over the hearth were almost the only words of sentiment which ever passed between those two about their plans. But from that moment those plans went forward more perfectly than if they had been talked over at every turn, and amended every day. That is the way with all true stories of hearth and home.

For instance, it was only that evening, when the day's work of all the six was done—and for boys and girls, it was hard work, too—Fanny and George would have been glad enough, both of them, to take each a book, and have the comfort of resting and reading. But George saw that the younger girls looked down-cast and heavy, and that the boys were whispering round the door-steps as if they wanted to go down to the blacksmith's shop by way of getting away from the sadness of the house. He hated to have them begin the habit of loafing there, with all the lazy boys and men from three miles round. And so he laid down his book, and said, as cheerily as if he had not laid his father's body in the grave the day before,—

"What shall we do to-night that we can all do together? Let us have something that we have never had before. Let us try what Mrs. Chisholm told us about. Let us act a ballad."

Of course the children were delighted with acting. George knew that, and Fanny looked across so gratefully to him, and laid her book away also; and, in a minute, Ethan, the young carpenter of the family, was putting up sconces for tallow candles to light the scenes, and Fanny had Sarah and Alice out in the wood-house, with the shawls, and the old ribbons, and strips of bright calico, which made up the dresses, and George instructed Walter as to the way in which he should arrange his armor and his horse, and so, after a period of preparation, which was much longer than the period of performance, they got ready to act in the kitchen the ballad of Lochinvar.

The children had a happy evening. They were frightened when they went to bed—the little ones—because they had been so merry. They came together with George and Fanny, and read their Bible as they had been used to do with their father, and the last text they read was, "Love is the fulfilling of the law." So the little ones went to bed, and left George and Fanny again together.

"Pretty hard, was it not?" said she, smiling through her tears. "But it is so much best for them that home should be the happiest place of all for them. After all, 'Love is the whole.'"

And that night's sacrifice, which the two older children made to the younger brothers and sisters as it were over their father's grave, was the beginning of many such nights, and of many other joint amusements which the children arranged together. They read Dickens aloud. They cleared out the corn-room at the end of the wood-house for a place for their dialogues and charades. The neighbors' children liked to come in, and, under very strict rules of early hours and of good behavior, they came. And George and Fanny found, not only that they were getting a reputation for keeping their own little flock in order, but that the nicest children all around were intrusted to their oversight, even by the most careful fathers and mothers. All this pleasure to the children came from the remembrance that "Love is the whole."

Far from finding themselves a lonely and forsaken family, these boys and girls soon found that they were surrounded with friends. George was quite right in assuming that he could manage the team, and could keep the little farm up, not to its full production under his father, but to a crop large enough to make them comfortable. Every little while there had to be a consultation. Mr. Snyder came down one day to offer him forty dollars a month and his board, if he would go off on a surveying party and carry chain for the engineers. It would be in a good line for promotion. Forty dollars a month to send home to Fanny was a great temptation. And George and Fanny put an extra pine-knot on the fire, after the children had gone to bed, that they might talk it over. But George declined the proposal, with many thanks to Mr. Snyder. He said to him, "that, if he went away, the whole household would be very much weakened. The boys could not carry on the farm alone, and would have to hire out. He thought they were too young for that. After all, Mr. Snyder, 'Love is the whole.'" And Mr. Snyder agreed with him.

Then, as a few years passed by, after another long council, in which another pine-knot was sacrificed on the hearth, and in which Walter assisted with George and Fanny, it was agreed that Walter should "hire out." He had "a chance," as they said, to go over to the Stacy Brothers, in the next county. Now the Stacy Brothers had the greatest stock farm in all that part of Illinois. They had to hire a great deal of help, and it was a great question to George and Fanny whether poor Walter might not get more harm than good there. But they told Walter perfectly frankly their doubts and their hopes. And he said boldly, "Never you fear me. Do you think I am such a fool as to forget? Do I not know that 'Love is the whole'? Shall I ever forget who taught us so?" And so it was determined that he should go.

Yes, and he went. The Stacys' great establishment was different indeed from the little cabin he had left. But the other boys there, and the men he met, Norwegians, Welshmen, Germans, Yankees, all sorts of people, all had hearts just like his heart. And a helpful boy, honest as a clock and brave as St. Paul, who really tried to serve every one as he found opportunity, made friends on the great stock farm just as he had in the corn-room at the end of the wood-house. And once a month, when their wages were paid, he was able to send home the lion's share of his to Fanny, in letters which every month were written a little better, and seemed a little more easy for him to write. And when Thanksgiving came, Mr. George Stacy sent him home for a fortnight, with a special message to his sister, "that he could not do without him, and he wished she would send him a dozen of such boys. He knew how to raise oxen, he said; but would Miss Fanny tell him how she brought up boys like Walter?"

"I could have told him," said Walter, "but I did not choose to; I could have told him that love was the whole."

And that story of Walter is only the story of the way in which Ethan also kept up the home tie, and came back, when he got a chance, from his voyages. His voyages were not on the sea. He "hired out" with a canal-boatman. Sometimes they went to the lake, and once they set sail there and came as far as Cleveland. Ethan made a great deal of fun in pretending to tell great sea-stories, like Swiss Family Robinson and Sinbad the Sailor. Fresh-water voyaging has its funny side, as has the deep-sea sailing. But Ethan did not hold to it long. His experience with grain brought him at last to Chicago, and he engaged there in the work of an elevator. But he lived always the old home life. There were three other boys he got acquainted with, one at Mr. Eggleston's church, one at the Custom House, and one at the place where he got his dinner, and they used to come up to his little room in the seventh story of the McKenzie House, and sit on his bed and in his chairs, just as the boys from the blacksmith's came into the corn-room. These four boys made a literary club "for reading Shakespeare and the British essayists." Often did they laugh afterwards at its title. They called it the Club of the Tetrarchy, because they thought it grand to have a Greek name. Whatever its name was, it kept them out of mischief. These boys grew up to be four ruling powers in Western life. And when, years after, some one asked Ethan how it was that he had so stanch a friend in Torrey, Ethan told the history of the seventh-story room at the McKenzie House, and he said, "Love is the whole."

Central in all his life was the little cabin of two rooms and a loft over it. There is no day of his life, from that time to this, of which Fanny cannot tell you the story from his weekly letters home. For though she does not live in the cabin now, she keeps the old letters filed and in order, and once a week steadily Ethan has written to her, and the letters are all sealed now with his own seal-ring, and on the seal-ring is carved the inscription, "Love is the whole."

I must not try to tell you the story of Alice's fortunes, or Sarah's. Every day of their lives was a romance, as is every day of yours and mine. Every day was a love-story, as may be every day of yours and mine, if we will make it so. As they all grew older their homes were all somewhat parted. The boys became men and married. The girls became women and married. George never pulled down the old farm-house, not even when he and Mr. Vaux built the beautiful house that stands next to it to-day. He put trellises on the sides of it. He trained cotoneaster and Roxbury wax-work over it. He carved a cross himself, and fastened it in the gable. Above the door, as you went in, was a picture of Mary Mother and her Child, with this inscription:—

> "Holy cell and holy shrine,
> For the Maid and Child divine!
> Remember, thou that seest her bending
>   O'er that babe upon her knee,
> All heaven is ever thus extending
>   Its arms of love round thee.
> Such love shall bless our archèd porch;
> Crowned with his cross, our cot becomes a church."

And in that little church he gathered the boys and girls of the neighborhood every Sunday afternoon, and told them stories and they sang together. And on the week days he got up children's parties there, which all the children thought rather the best experiences of the week, and he and his wife and his own children grew to think the hours in the cabin the best hours of all. There were pictures on the walls; they painted the windows themselves with flower-pictures, and illuminated them with colored leaves. But there were but two inscriptions. These were over the inside of the two doors, and both inscriptions were the same,—"Love is the whole."

They told all these stories, and a hundred more, at a great Thanksgiving party after the war. Walter and his wife and his children came from Sangamon County; and the General and all his family came down from Winetka; and Fanny and the Governor and all their seven came all the way from Minnesota; and Alice and her husband and all her little ones came up the river, and so across from Quincy; and Sarah and Gilbert, with the twins and the babies, came in their own carriage all the way from Horace. So there was a Thanksgiving dinner set for all the six, and the six husbands and wives, and the twenty-seven children. In twenty years, since their father died, those brothers and sisters had lived for each other. They had had separate houses, but they had spent the money in them for each other. No one of them had said that anything he had was his own. They had confided wholly each in each. They had passed through much sorrow, and in that sorrow had strengthened each other. They had passed through much joy, and the joy had been multiplied tenfold because it was joy that was shared. At the Thanksgiving they acted the ballad of Lochinvar again, or rather some of the children did. And that set Fanny the oldest and Sarah the youngest to telling to the oldest nephews and nieces some of the stories of the cabin days. But Fanny said, when the children asked for more, "There is no need of any more,—'Love is the whole.'"

Christmas and Rome

The first Christmas this in which a Roman Senate has sat in Rome since the old-fashioned Roman Senates went under,—or since they "went up," if we take the expressive language of our Chicago friends.

And Pius IX. is celebrating Christmas with an uncomfortable look backward, and an uncomfortable look forward, and an uncomfortable look all around. It is a suggestive matter, this Italian Parliament sitting in Rome. It suggests a good deal of history and a good deal of prophecy.

"They say" (whoever they may be) that somewhere in Rome there is a range of portraits of popes, running down from never so far back; that only one niche was left in the architecture, which received the portrait of Pius IX., and that then that place was full. Maybe it is so. I did not see the row. But I have heard the story a thousand times. Be it true, be it false, there are, doubtless, many other places where portraits of coming popes could be hung. There is a little wall-room left in the City Hall of New York. There are, also, other palaces in which popes could live. Palaces are as plenty in America as are Pullman cars. But it is possible that there are no such palaces in Rome.

So this particular Christmas sets one careering back a little, to look at that mysterious connection of Rome with Christianity, which has held on so steadily since the first Christmas got itself put on historical record by a Roman census-maker. Humanly speaking, it was nothing more nor less than a Roman census which makes the word Bethlehem to be a sacred word over all the world to-day. To any person who sees the humorous contrasts of history there is reason for a bit of a smile when he thinks of the way this census came into being, and then remembers what came of it. Here was a consummate movement of Augustus, who would fain have the statistics of his empire. Such excellent things are statistics! "You can prove anything by statistics," says Mr. Canning, "except—the truth." So Augustus orders his census, and his census is taken. This Quirinus, or Quirinius, pro-consul of Syria, was the first man who took it there, says the Bible. Much appointing of marshals and deputy-marshals,—men good at counting, and good at writing, and good at collecting fees! Doubtless it was a great staff achievement of Quirinus, and made much talk in its time. And it is so well condensed at last and put into tables with indexes and averages as to be very creditable, I will not doubt, to the census bureau. But alas! as time rolls on, things change, so that this very Quirinus, who with all a pro-consul's power took such pains to record for us the number of people there were in Bethlehem and in Judah, would have been clean forgotten himself, and his census too, but that things turned bottom upward. The meanest child born in Bethlehem when this census business was going on happened to prove to be King of the World. It happened that he overthrew the dynasty of Cæsar Augustus, and his

temples, and his empire. It happened that everything which was then established tottered and fell, as the star of this child arose. And the child's star did
rise. And now this Publius Sulpicius Quirinus or Quirinius,—a great man in
his day, for whom Augustus asked for a triumph,—is rescued from complete
forgetfulness because that baby happened to be born in Syria when his census
was going on!

I always liked to think that some day when Augustus Cæsar was on a
state visit to the Temple of Fortune some attentive clerk handed him down
the roll which had just come in and said, "From Syria, your Highness!" that
he might have a chance to say something to the Emperor; that the Emperor
thanked him, and, in his courtly way, opened the roll so as to seem inter-
ested; that his eye caught the words "Bethlehem—village near Jerusalem,"
and the figures which showed the number of the people and of the children
and of all the infants there. Perhaps. No matter if not. Sixty years after,
Augustus' successor, Nero, set fire to Rome in a drunken fit. The Temple of
Fortune caught the flames, and our roll, with Bethlehem and the count of
Joseph's possessions twisted and crackled like any common rag, turned to
smoke and ashes, and was gone. That is what such statistics come to!

Five hundred years after, the whole scene is changed. The Church of
Christ, which for hundreds of years worshipped under-ground in Rome,
has found air and sunlight now. It is almost five hundred years after Paul
enters Rome as a prisoner, after Nero burned Rome down, that a monk of St.
Andrew, one of the more prominent monasteries of the city of Rome, walking through that great market-place of the city—which to this hour preserves
most distinctly, perhaps, the memory of what Rome was—saw a party of
fair-haired slaves for sale among the rest. He stops to ask where they come
from, and of what nation they are; to be told they are "Angli." "Rather Angeli,"
says Gregory,—"rather angels;" and with other sacred *bon-mots* he fixes the
pretty boys and pretty girls in his memory. Nor are these familiar plays upon
words to be spoken of as mere puns. Gregory was determined to attempt the
conversion of the land from which these "angels" came. He started on the
pilgrimage, which was then a dangerous one; but was recalled by the pope of
his day, at the instance of his friends, who could not do without him.

A few years more and this monk is Bishop of Rome. True to the promise of
the market-place, he organizes the Christian mission which fulfils his prophecy. He sends Austin with his companions to the island of the fair-haired slave
boys; and that new step in the civilization of that land comes, to which we owe
it that we are met in this church, nay, that we live in this land this day.

So far has the star of the baby of Bethlehem risen in a little more than five
centuries. A Christian dominion has laid its foundations in the Eternal City.
And you and I, gentle reader, are what we are and are where we are because that
monk of St. Andrew saw those angel boys that day in a Roman market-place.

The Survivor's Story

ortunately we were with our wives.

It is in general an excellent custom, as I will explain if opportunity is given.

First, you are thus sure of good company.

For four mortal hours we had ground along, and stopped and waited and started again, in the drifts between Westfield and Springfield. We had shrieked out our woes by the voices of fire-engines. Brave men had dug. Patient men had sate inside, and waited for the results of the digging. At last, in triumph, at eleven and three-quarters, as they say in Cinderella, we entered the Springfield station.

It was Christmas eve!

Leaving the train to its devices, Blatchford and his wife (her name was Sarah), and I with mine (her name was Phebe), walked quickly with our little sacks out of the station, ploughed and waded along the white street, not to the Massasoit,—no, but to the old Eagle and Star, which was still standing, and was a favorite with us youngsters. Good waffles, maple syrup *ad lib.*, such fixings of other sorts as we preferred, and some liberty. The amount of liberty in absolutely first-class hotels is but small. A drowsy boy waked, and turned up the gas. Blatchford entered our names on the register, and cried at once, "By George, Wolfgang is here, and Dick! What luck!" for Dick and Wolfgang also travel with their wives. The boy explained that they had come up the river in the New-Haven train, were only nine hours behind time, had arrived at ten, and had just finished supper and gone to bed. We ordered rare beef-steak, waffles, dip-toast, omelettes with kidneys, and omelettes without; we toasted our feet at the open fire in the parlor; we ate the supper when it was ready; and we also went to bed; rejoicing that we had home with us, having travelled with our wives; and that we could keep our merry Christmas here. If only Wolfgang and Dick and their wives would join us, all would be well. (Wolfgang's wife was named Bertha, and Dick's was named Hosanna,—a name I have never met with elsewhere.)

Bed followed; and I am a graceless dog that I do not write a sonnet here on the unbroken slumber that followed. Breakfast, by arrangement of us four, at nine. At 9.30, to us enter Bertha, Dick, Hosanna, and Wolfgang, to name them in alphabetical order. Four chairs had been turned down for them. Four chops, four omelettes, and four small oval dishes of fried potatoes had been ordered, and now appeared. Immense shouting, immense kissing among those who had that privilege, general wondering, and great congratulating that our wives were there. Solid resolution that we would advance no farther. Here, and here only, in Springfield itself, would we celebrate our Christmas day.

It may be remarked in parenthesis that we had learned already that no train had entered the town since eleven and a quarter; and it was known by telegraph that none was within thirty-four miles and a half of the spot, at the moment the vow was made.

We waded and ploughed our way through the snow to church. I think Mr. Rumfry, if that is the gentleman's name who preached an admirable Christmas sermon, in a beautiful church there is, will remember the platoon of four men and four women, who made perhaps a fifth of his congregation in that storm,—a storm which shut off most church-going. Home again; a jolly fire in the parlor, dry stockings, and dry slippers. Turkeys, and all things fitting for the dinner; and then a general assembly, not in a caravanserai, not in a coffee-room, but in the regular guests' parlor of a New-England second-class hotel, where, as it was ordered, there were no "transients" but ourselves that day; and whence all the "boarders" had gone either to their own rooms, or to other homes.

For people who have their wives with them, it is not difficult to provide entertainment on such an occasion.

"Bertha," said Wolfgang, "could you not entertain us with one of your native dances?"

"Ho! slave," said Dick to Hosanna, "play upon the virginals." And Hosanna played a lively Arab air on the tavern piano, while the fair Bertha danced with a spirit unusual. Was it indeed in memory of the Christmas of her own dear home in Circassia?

All that, from "Bertha" to "Circassia," is not so. We did not do this at all. That was all a slip of the pen. What we did was this. John Blatchford pulled the bell-cord till it broke (they always break in novels, and sometimes they do in taverns). This bell-cord broke. The sleepy boy came; and John said, "Caitiff, is there never a barber in the house?" The frightened boy said there was; and John bade him send him. In a minute the barber appeared,—black, as was expected,—with a shining face, and white teeth, and in shirt sleeves, and broad grins. "Do you tell me, Cæsar," said John, "that in your country they do not wear their coats on Christmas day?"—"Sartin, they do, sir, when they go out doors."

"Do you tell me, Cæsar," said Dick, "that they have doors in your country?"—"Sartin, they do," said poor Cæsar, flurried.

"Boy," said I, "the gentlemen are making fun of you. They want to know if you ever keep Christmas in your country without a dance."

"Never, sar," said poor Cæsar.

"Do they dance without music?"

"No, sar; never."

"Go, then," I said in my sternest accents,—"go fetch a zittern, or a banjo, or a kit, or a hurdy-gurdy, or a fiddle."

The black boy went, and returned with his violin. And as the light grew gray, and crept into the darkness, and as the darkness gathered more thick and more, he played for us and he played for us, tune after tune; and we danced,—first with precision, then in sport, then in wild holiday frenzy. We began with waltzes,—so great is the convenience of travelling with your wives,—where should we have been, had we been all sole alone, four men? Probably playing whist or euchre. And now we began with waltzes, which passed into polkas, which subsided into round dances; and then in very exhaustion we fell back in a grave quadrille. I danced with Hosanna; Wolfgang and Sarah were our *vis-à-vis*. We went through the same set that Noah and his three boys danced in the ark with their four wives, and which has been danced ever since, in every moment, on one or another spot of the dry earth, going round it with the sun, like the drumbeat of England,—right and left, first two forward, right hand across, *pastorale*,—the whole series of them; we did them with as much spirit as if it had been on a flat on the side of Ararat, ground yet too muddy for croquet. Then Blatchford called for "Virginia Reel," and we raced and chased through that. Poor Cæsar began to get exhausted, but a little flip from down stairs helped him amazingly. And, after the flip, Dick cried, "Can you not dance 'Money-Musk'?" And in one wild frenzy of delight we danced "Money-Musk" and "Hull's Victory" and "Dusty Miller" and "Youth's Companion," and "Irish Jigs" on the closet-door lifted off for the occasion, till the men lay on the floor screaming with the fun, and the women fell back on the sofas, fairly faint with laughing.

All this last, since the sentence after "Circassia," is a mistake. There was not any bell, nor any barber, and we did not dance at all. This was all a slip of my memory.

What we really did was this:—

John Blatchford said,—"Let us all tell stories." It was growing dark and he had put more logs on the fire.

Bertha said,—

"Heap on more wood, the wind is chill;

But let it whistle as it will,

We'll keep our merry Christmas still."

She said that because it was in "Bertha's Visit," a very stupid book which she remembered.

Then Wolfgang told

THE PENNY-A-LINER'S STORY

[Wolfgang is a reporter, or was then, on the staff of the "Star."]

When I was on the "Tribune" (he never was on the "Tribune" an hour, unless he calls selling the "Tribune" at Fort Plains being on the "Tribune"). But I tell the story as he told it. He said,—

When I was on the "Tribune," I was despatched to report Mr. Webster's great reply to Hayne. This was in the days of stages. We had to ride from

Baltimore to Washington early in the morning to get there in time. I found my boots were gone from my room when the stage-man called me, and I reported that speech in worsted slippers my wife had given me the week before. As we came into Bladensburg it grew light, and I recognized my boots on the feet of my fellow-passenger,—there was but one other man in the stage. I turned to claim them, but stopped in a moment, for it was Webster himself. How serene his face looked as he slept there! He woke soon, passed the time of day, offered me a part of a sandwich,—for we were old friends,—I was counsel against him in the Ogden case. Said Webster to me,—"Steele, I am bothered about this speech: I have a paragraph in it which I cannot word up to my mind." And he repeated it to me. "How would this do?" said he. "'Let us hope that the sense of unrestricted freedom may be so intertwined with the desire to preserve a connection of the several parts of the body politic, that some arrangement, more or less lasting, may prove in a measure satisfactory.' How would that do?"

I said I liked the idea, but the expression seemed involved.

"And it is involved," said Webster; "but I can't improve it."

"How would this do?" said I.

"'Liberty and Union, now and forever, one and inseparable!'"

"Capital!" he said, "capital! write that down for me." At that moment we arrived at the Capitol steps. I wrote down the words for him, and from my notes he read them, when that place in the speech came along.

All of us applauded the story.

Phebe then told

The Schoolmistress's Story

You remind me of the impression that very speech made on me, as I heard Henry Chapin deliver it at an exhibition at Leicester Academy. I resolved then that I would free the slave, or perish in the attempt. But how? I, a woman,—disfranchised by the law? Ha! I saw!

I went to Arkansas. I opened a "Normal College, or Academy for Teachers." We had balls every second night, to make it popular. Immense numbers came. Half the teachers of the Southern States were trained there. I had admirable instructors in Oil Painting and Music,—the most essential studies. The Arithmetic I taught myself. I taught it well. I achieved fame. I achieved wealth; invested in Arkansas Five per Cents. Only one secret device I persevered in. To all,—old and young, innocent girls and sturdy men,—I so taught the multiplication-table, that one fatal error was hidden in its array of facts. The nine line is the difficult one. I buried the error there. "Nine times six," I taught them, "is fifty-six." The rhyme made it easy. The gilded falsehood passed from lip to lip, from

State to State,—one little speck in a chain of golden verity. I retired from teaching. Slowly I watched the growth of the rebellion. At last the aloe blossom shot up,—after its hundred years of waiting. The Southern heart was fired. I brooded over my revenge. I repaired to Richmond. I opened a first-class boarding-house, where all the Cabinet, and most of the Senate, came for their meals; and I had eight permanents. Soon their brows clouded. The first flush of victory passed away. Night after night, they sat over their calculations, which all came wrong. I smiled,—and was a villain! None of their sums would prove. None of their estimates matched the performance! Never a muster-roll that fitted as it should do! And I,—the despised boarding-mistress,—I alone knew why! Often and often, when Memminger has said to me, with an oath, "Why this discordancy in our totals?" have my lips burned to tell the secret! But no! I hid it in my bosom. And when, at last, I saw a black regiment march into Richmond, singing "John Brown," I cried, for the first time in twenty years, "Nine times six is fifty-four;" and gloated in my sweet revenge.

Then was hushed the harp of Phebe, and Dick told his story.

THE INSPECTOR OF GAS-METERS' STORY

Mine is a tale of the ingratitude of republics. It is well-nigh thirty years since I was walking by the Owego and Ithaca Railroad,—a crooked road, not then adapted to high speed. Of a sudden I saw that a long cross timber, on a trestle, high above a swamp, had sprung up from its ties. I looked for a spike with which to secure it. I found a stone with which to hammer the spike. But, at this moment, a train approached, down hill. I screamed. They heard! But the engine had no power to stop the heavy train. With the presence of mind of a poet, and the courage of a hero, I flung my own weight on the fatal timber. I would hold it down, or perish. The engine came. The elasticity of the pine timber whirled me in the air! But I held on. The tender crossed. Again I was flung in wild gyrations. But I held on. "It is no bed of roses," I said; "but what act of Parliament was there that I should be happy." Three passenger cars, and ten freight cars, as was then the vicious custom of that road, passed me. But I held on, repeating to myself texts of Scripture to give me courage. As the last car passed, I was whirled into the air by the rebound of the rafter. "Heavens!" I said, "if my orbit is a hyperbola, I shall never return to earth." Hastily I estimated its ordinates, and calculated the curve. What bliss! It was a parabola! After a flight of a hundred and seventeen cubits, I landed, head down, in a soft mud-hole.

In that train was the young U. S. Grant, on his way to West Point for examination. But for me the armies of the Republic would have had no leader.

I pressed my claim, when I asked to be appointed to England. Although no one else wished to go, I alone was forgotten. Such is gratitude with republics!

He ceased. Then Sarah Blatchford told

THE WHEELER AND WILSON'S OPERATIVE'S STORY

My father had left the anchorage of Sorrento for a short voyage, if voyage it may be called. Life was young, and this world seemed heaven. The yacht bowled on under close-reefed stay-sails, and all was happy. Suddenly the corsairs seized us: all were slain in my defence; but I,—this fatal gift of beauty bade them spare my life!

Why linger on my tale! In the Zenana of the Shah of Persia I found my home. "How escape his eye?" I said; and, fortunately, I remembered that in my reticule I carried one box of F. Kidder's indelible ink. Instantly I applied the liquid in the large bottle to one cheek. Soon as it was dry, I applied that in the small bottle, and sat in the sun one hour. My head ached with the sunlight, but what of that? I was a fright, and I knew all would be well.

I was consigned, so soon as my hideous deficiencies were known, to the sewing-room. Then how I sighed for my machine! Alas! it was not there; but I constructed an imitation from a cannon-wheel, a coffee-mill, and two nut-crackers. And with this I made the under-clothing for the palace and the Zenana.

I also vowed revenge. Nor did I doubt one instant how; for in my youth I had read Lucretia Borgia's memoirs, and I had a certain rule for slowly slaying a tyrant at a distance. I was in charge of the shah's own linen. Every week, I set back the buttons on his shirt collars by the width of one thread; or, by arts known to me, I shrunk the binding of the collar by a like proportion. Tighter and tighter with each week did the vice close around his larynx. Week by week, at the high religious festivals, I could see his face was blacker and blacker. At length the hated tyrant died. The leeches called it apoplexy. I did not undeceive them. His guards sacked the palace. I bagged the diamonds, fled with them to Trebizond, and sailed thence in a caïque to South Boston. No more! such memories oppress me.

Her voice was hushed. I told my tale in turn.

THE CONDUCTOR'S STORY

I was poor. Let this be my excuse, or rather my apology. I entered a Third Avenue car at Thirty-sixth Street, and saw the conductor sleeping. Satan tempted me, and I took from him his badge, 213. I see the hated figures now. When he woke, he knew not he had lost it. The car started, and he walked to the rear. With the badge on my coat, I collected eight fares within, stepped forward, and sprang into the street. Poverty is my only apology for the crime. I concealed myself in a cellar where men were playing with props. Fear is my only excuse. Lest they should suspect me, I joined their game, and my forty cents were soon three dollars and seventy. With these ill-gotten gains, I visited the gold exchange, then open evenings. My superior intelligence enabled me to place well my modest means, and at midnight I had a competence. Let me be a warning to all young men. Since that night, I have never gambled more.

I threw the hated badge into the river. I bought a palace on Murray Hill, and led an upright and honorable life. But since that night of terror the sound of the horse-cars oppresses me. Always since, to go up town or down, I order my own coupé, with George to drive me; and never have I entered the cleanly, sweet, and airy carriage provided for the public. I cannot; conscience is too much for me. You see in me a monument of crime.

I said no more. A moment's pause, a few natural tears, and a single sigh hushed the assembly; then Bertha, with her siren voice, told—

THE WIFE F BIDDEFORD'S STORY

At the time you speak of, I was the private governess of two lovely boys, Julius and Pompey,—Pompey the senior of the two. The black-eyed darling! I see him now. I also see, hanging to his neck, his blue-eyed brother, who had given Pompey his black eye the day before. Pompey was generous to a fault; Julius, parsimonious beyond virtue. I therefore instructed them in two different rooms. To Pompey, I read the story of "Waste not, want not." To Julius, on the other hand, I spoke of the All-love of his great Mother Nature, and her profuse gifts to her children. Leaving him with grapes and oranges, I stepped back to Pompey, and taught him how to untie parcels so as to save the string. Leaving him winding the string neatly, I went back to Julius, and gave to him ginger-cakes. The dear boys grew from year to year. They outgrew their knickerbockers, and had trousers. They outgrew their jackets, and became men; and I felt that I had not lived in vain. I had conquered nature. Pompey, the little spendthrift, was the honored cashier of a savings bank, till he ran away with the capital. Julius, the miser, became the chief croupier at the New Crockford's. One of those boys is now in Botany Bay, and the other is in Sierra Leone!

"I thought you were going to say in a hotter place," said John Blatchford; and he told his story:—

THE STOKER'S STORY

We were crossing the Atlantic in a Cunarder. I was second stoker on the starboard watch. In that horrible gale we spoke of before dinner, the coal was exhausted, and I, as the best-dressed man, was sent up to the captain to ask what we should do. I found him himself at the wheel. He almost cursed me and bade me say nothing of coal, at a moment when he must keep her head to the wind with her full power, or we were lost. He bade me slide my hand into his pocket, and take out the key of the after freight-room, open that, and use the contents for fuel. I returned hastily to the engine-room, and we did as we were bid. The room contained nothing but old account books, which made a hot and effective fire.

On the third day the captain came down himself into the engine-room, where I had never seen him before, called me aside, and told me that by mistake he had given me the wrong key; asking me if I had used it. I pointed to him the empty room: not a leaf was left. He turned pale with fright. As I saw his emotion he confided to me the truth. The books were the evidences or accounts of the British national debt; of what is familiarly known as the Consolidated Fund, or the "Consols." They had been secretly sent to New York for the examination of James Fiske, who had been asked to advance a few millions on this security to the English Exchequer, and now all evidence of indebtedness was gone!

The captain was about to leap into the sea. But I dissuaded him. I told him to say nothing; I would keep his secret; no man else knew it. The Government would never utter it. It was safe in our hands. He reconsidered his purpose. We came safe to port and did—nothing.

Only on the first quarter-day which followed, I obtained leave of absence, and visited the Bank of England, to see what happened. At the door was this placard,—"Applicants for dividends will file a written application, with name and amount, at desk A, and proceed in turn to the Paying Teller's Office." I saw their ingenuity. They were making out new books, certain that none would apply but those who were accustomed to. So skilfully do men of Government study human nature.

I stepped lightly to one of the public desks. I took one of the blanks. I filled it out, "John Blatchford, £1747 6s. 8d.," and handed it in at the open trap. I took my place in the queue in the teller's room. After an agreeable hour, a pile, not thick, of Bank of England notes was given to me; and since that day I have quarterly drawn that amount from the maternal government of that country. As I left the teller's room, I observed the captain in the queue. He was the seventh man from the window, and I have never seen him more.

We then asked Hosanna for her story.

THE N. E. HISTORICAL GENEALOGIST'S STORY

"My story," said she, "will take us far back into the past. It will be necessary for me to dwell on some incidents in the first settlement of this country, and I propose that we first prepare and enjoy the Christmas-tree. After this, if your courage holds, you shall hear an over-true tale." Pretty creature, how little she knew what was before us!

As we had sat listening to the stories, we had been preparing for the tree. Shopping being out of the question, we were fain from our own stores to make up our presents, while the women were arranging nuts, and blown egg-shells, and pop-corn strings from the stores of the "Eagle and Star." The popping of corn in two corn-poppers had gone on through the whole of the story-telling. All being so nearly ready, I called the drowsy boy again, and, showing him a very large stick in the wood-box, asked him to bring me a hatchet. To my great joy he brought the axe of the establishment, and I bade him farewell. How little did he think what was before him! So soon as he had gone I went stealthily down the stairs, and stepping out into the deep snow, in front of the hotel, looked up into the lovely night. The storm had ceased, and I could see far back into the heavens. In the still evening my strokes might have been heard far and wide, as I cut down one of the two pretty Norways that shaded Mr. Pynchon's front walk, next the hotel. I dragged it over the snow. Blatchford and Steele lowered sheets to me from the large parlor window, which I attached to the larger end of the tree. With infinite difficulty they hauled it in. I joined them in the parlor, and soon we had as stately a tree growing there as was in any home of joy that night in the river counties.

With swift fingers did our wives adorn it. I should have said above, that we travelled with our wives, and that I would recommend that custom to others. It was impossible, under the circumstances, to maintain much secrecy; but it had been agreed that all who wished to turn their backs to the circle, in the preparation of presents, might do so without offence to the others. As the presents were wrapped, one by one, in paper of different colors, they were marked with the names of giver and receiver, and placed in a large clothes-basket. At last all was done. I had wrapped up my knife, my pencil-case, my letter-case, for Steele, Blatchford, and Dick. To my wife I gave my gold watch-key, which fortunately fits her watch; to Hosanna, a mere trifle, a seal ring I wore; to Bertha, my gold chain; and to Sarah Blatchford, the watch which generally hung from it. For a few moments, we retired to our rooms while the pretty Hosanna arranged the forty-nine presents on the tree. Then she clapped her hands, and we rushed in. What a wondrous sight! What a shout of infantine laughter and charming prattle! for in that happy moment were we not all children again?

I see my story hurries to its close. Dick, who is the tallest, mounted a step-ladder, and called us by name to receive our presents. I had a nice gold watch-key from Hosanna, a knife from Steele, a letter-case from Phebe, and a pretty pencil-case from Bertha. Dick had given me his watch-chain, which he knew I fancied; Sarah Blatchford, a little toy of a Geneva watch she wore; and her husband, a handsome seal ring, a present to him from the Czar, I believe; Phebe, that is my wife,—for we were travelling with our wives,—had a pencil-case from Steele, a pretty little letter-case from

Dick, a watch-key from me, and a French repeater from Blatchford; Sarah Blatchford gave her the knife she carried, with some bright verses, saying that it was not to cut love; Bertha, a watch-chain; and Hosanna a ring of turquoise and amethysts. The other presents were similar articles, and were received, as they were given, with much tender feeling. But at this moment, as Dick was on the top of the flight of steps, handing down a red apple from the tree, a slight catastrophe occurred.

The first I was conscious of was the angry hiss of steam. In a moment I perceived that the steam-boiler, from which the tavern was warmed, had exploded. The floor beneath us rose, and we were driven with it through the ceiling and the rooms above,—through an opening in the roof into the still night. Around us in the air were flying all the other contents and occupants of the Star and Eagle. How bitterly was I reminded of Dick's flight from the railroad track of the Ithaca & Owego Railroad! But I could not hope such an escape as his. Still my flight was in a parabola; and, in a period not longer than it has taken to describe it, I was thrown senseless, at last, into a deep snow-bank near the United States Arsenal.

Tender hands lifted me and assuaged me. Tender teams carried me to the City Hospital. Tender eyes brooded over me. Tender science cared for me. It proved necessary, before I recovered, to amputate my two legs at the hips. My right arm was wholly removed, by a delicate and curious operation, from the socket. We saved the stump of my left arm, which was amputated just below the shoulder. I am still in the hospital to recruit my strength. The doctor does not like to have me occupy my mind at all; but he says there is no harm in my compiling my memoirs, or writing magazine stories. My faithful nurse has laid me on my breast on a pillow, has put a camel's-hair pencil in my mouth, and, feeling almost personally acquainted with John Carter, the artist, I have written out for you, in his method, the story of my last Christmas.

I am sorry to say that the others have never been found.

The Same Christmas in Old England and New

T he first Christmas in New England was celebrated by some people who tried as hard as they could not to celebrate it at all. But looking back on that year 1620, the first year when Christmas was celebrated in New England, I cannot find that anybody got up a better *fête* than did these Lincolnshire weavers and ploughmen who had got a little taste of Dutch firmness, and resolved on that particular day, that, whatever else happened to them, they would not celebrate Christmas at all.

Here is the story as William Bradford tells it:

"Ye 16. *day* ye winde came faire, and they arrived safe in this harbor. And after wards tooke better view of ye place, and resolved wher to pitch their dwelling; and ye 25. *day* begane to erecte ye first house for comone use to receive them and their goods."

You see, dear reader, that when on any 21st or 22d of December you give the children parched corn, and let them pull candy and swim candles in nut-shells in honor of the "landing of the Forefathers"—if by good luck you be of Yankee blood, and do either of these praiseworthy things—you are not celebrating the anniversary of the day when the women and children landed, wrapped up in water-proofs, with the dog and John Carver in headpiece, and morion, as you have seen in many pictures. That all came afterward. Be cool and self-possessed, and I will guide you through the whole chronology safely—Old Style and New Style, first landing and second landing, Sabbaths and Sundays, Carver's landing and Mary Chilton's landing, so that you shall know as much as if you had fifteen ancestors, a cradle, a tankard, and an oak chest in the Mayflower, and you shall come out safely and happily at the first Christmas day.

Know then, that when the poor Mayflower at last got across the Atlantic, Massachusetts stretched out her right arm to welcome her, and she came to anchor as early as the 11th of November in Provincetown Harbor. This was the day when the compact of the cabin of the Mayflower was signed, when the fiction of the "social compact" was first made real. Here they fitted their shallop, and in this shallop, on the sixth of December, ten of the Pilgrims and six of the ship's crew sailed on their exploration. They came into Plymouth harbor on the tenth, rested on Watson's island on the eleventh,—which was Sunday,—and on Monday, the twelfth, landed on the mainland, stepping on Plymouth rock and marching inland to explore the country. Add now nine days to this date for the difference then existing between Old Style and New Style, and you come upon the twenty-first of December, which is the day you ought to celebrate as Forefathers' Day. On that day give the children parched corn in token of the new provant, the English walnut in token of the old, and send them to bed with Elder Brewster's name, Mary Chilton's, Edward Winslow's, and John Billington's, to dream upon. Observe still that only these ten men have landed. All the women and children and the other men are over in Provincetown harbor. These ten, liking the country well enough, go across the bay to Provincetown where they find poor Bradford's wife drowned in their absence, and bring the ship across into Plymouth harbor on the sixteenth. Now you will say of course that they were so glad to get here that they began to build at once; but you are entirely mistaken, for they did not do any such thing. There was a little of the John Bull about them and a little of the Dutchman. The seventeenth was Sunday. Of course they could not build a city on Sunday. Monday they explored, and Tuesday they explored more. Wednesday,

"After we had called on God for direction, we came to this resolution, to go presently ashore again, and to take a better view of two places, which we thought most fitting for us; for we could not now take time for further search or consideration, our victuals being much spent, especially our beer."

Observe, this is the Pilgrims' or Forefathers' beer, and not the beer of the ship, of which there was still some store. Acting on this resolution they went ashore again, and concluded by "most voices" to build Plymouth where Plymouth now is. One recommendation seems to have been that there was a good deal of land already clear. But this brought with it the counter difficulty that they had to go half a quarter of a mile for their wood. So there they left twenty people on shore, resolving the next day to come and build their houses. But the next day it stormed, and the people on shore had to come back to the ship, and Richard Britteridge died. And Friday it stormed so that they could not land, and the people on the shallop who had gone ashore the day before could not get back to the ship. Saturday was the twenty-third, as they counted, and some of them got ashore and cut timber and carried it to be ready for building. But they reserved their forces still, and Sunday, the twenty-fourth, no one worked of course. So that when Christmas day came, the day which every man, woman and child of them had been trained to regard as a holy day—as a day specially given to festivity and specially exempted from work, all who could went on shore and joined those who had landed already. So that William Bradford was able to close the first book of his history by saying: "Ye 25. *day* begane to erect ye first house for comone use to receive them and their goods."

Now, this all may have been accidental. I do not say it was not. But when I come to the record of Christmas for next year and find that Bradford writes: "One ye day called Chrismas-day, ye Gov'r caled them out to worke (as was used)," I cannot help thinking that the leaders had a grim feeling of satisfaction in "secularizing" the first Christmas as thoroughly as they did. They wouldn't work on Sunday, and they would work on Christmas.

They did their best to desecrate Christmas, and they did it by laying one of the cornerstones of an empire.

Now, if the reader wants to imagine the scene,—the Christmas celebration or the Christmas desecration, he shall call it which he will, according as he is Roman or Puritan himself,—I cannot give him much material to spin his thread from. Here is the little story in the language of the time:

"Munday the 25. day, we went on shore, some to fell tymber, some to saw, some to riue, and some to carry, so no man rested all that day, but towards night some as they were at worke, heard a noyse of some Indians, which caused vs all to goe to our Muskets, but we heard no further, so we came aboord againe, and left some twentie to keepe the court of gard; that night we had a sore storme of winde and rayne.

"Munday the 25. being Christmas day, we began to drinke water aboord, but at night the Master caused vs to have some Beere, and so on board we had diverse times now and then some Beere, but on shore none at all."

There is the story as it is told by the only man who chose to write it down. Let us not at this moment go into an excursus to inquire who he was and who he was not. Only diligent investigation has shown beside that this first house was about twenty feet square, and that it was for their common use to receive them and their goods. The tradition says that it was on the south side of what is now Leyden street, near the declivity of the hill. What it was, I think no one pretends to say absolutely. I am of the mind of a dear friend of mine, who used to say that, in the hardships of those first struggles, these old forefathers of ours, as they gathered round the fires (which they did have—no Christian Registers for them to warm their cold hands by), used to pledge themselves to each other in solemn vows that they would leave to posterity no detail of the method of their lives. Posterity should not make pictures out of them, or, if it did, should make wrong ones; which accordingly, posterity has done. What was the nature, then, of this twenty-foot-square store-house, in which, afterward, they used to sleep pretty compactly, no man can say. Dr. Young suggests a log cabin, but I do not believe that the log cabin was yet invented. I think it is more likely that the Englishmen rigged their two-handled saws,—after the fashion known to readers of Sanford and Merton in an after age,—and made plank for themselves. The material for imagination, as far as costume goes, may be got from the back of a fifty-dollar national bank-note, which the well-endowed reader will please take from his pocket, or from a roll of Lorillard's tobacco at his side, on which he will find the good reduction of Weir's admirable picture of the embarkation. Or, if the reader has been unsuccessful in his investment in Lorillard, he will find upon the back of the one-dollar bank-note a reduced copy of the fresco of the "Landing" in the Capitol, which will answer his purpose equally well. Forty or fifty Englishmen, in hats and doublets and hose of that fashion, with those odd English axes that you may see in your Æsop's fable illustrations, and with their double-handled saws, with a few beetles, and store of wedges, must make up your tableau, dear reader. Make it *vivant*, if you can.

To help myself in the matter, I sometimes group them on the bank there just above the brook,—you can see the place to-day, if it will do you any good—at some moment when the women have come ashore to see how the work goes on—and remembering that Mrs. Hemans says "they sang"—I throw the women all in a chorus of soprano and contralto voices on the left, Mrs. Winslow and Mrs. Carver at their head, Mrs. W. as *prima assoluta soprano* and Mrs. Carver as *prima assoluta contralto*,—I range on the right the men with W. Bradford and W. Brewster as leaders—and between, facing us, the audience,—who are lower down in the valley of the brook, I place Giovanni Carver (tenor) and Odoardo Winslow (basso) and have them sing in the English dialect of their day,

Suoni la tromba,

Carver waving the red-cross flag of England, and Winslow swinging a broadaxe above his head in similar revolutions. The last time I saw any Puritans doing this at the opera, one had a star-spangled banner and the other an Italian tricolor,—but I am sure my placing on the stage is more accurate than that. But I find it very hard to satisfy myself that this is the correct idealization. Yet Mrs. Hemans says the songs were "songs of lofty cheer," which precisely describes the duet in Puritani.

It would be an immense satisfaction, if by palimpsest under some old cash-book of that century, or by letters dug out from some family collection in England, one could just discover that "John Billington, having become weary with cutting down a small fir-tree which had been allotted to him, took his snaphance and shot with him, and calling a dog he had, to whom in the Low Countries the name Crab had been given, went after fowle. Crossing the brook and climbing up the bank to an open place which was there, he found what had been left by the savages of one of their gardens,—and on the ground, picking at the stalkes of the corne, a flocke of large blacke birds such as he had never seen before. His dogge ran at them and frightened them, and they all took wing heavily, but not so quick but that Billington let fly at them and brought two of them down,—one quite dead and one hurt so badly that he could not fly. Billington killed them both and tyed them together, and following after the flocke had another shot at them, and by a good Providence hurte three more. He tyed two of these together and brought the smallest back to us, not knowing what he brought, being but a poor man and ignorant. Hee is but a lazy Fellowe, and was sore tired with the weight of his burden, which was nigh fortie pounds. Soe soon as he saw it, the Governour and the rest knew that it was a wild Turkie, and albeit he chid Billington sharply, he sent four men with him, as it were Calebs and Joshuas, to bring in these firstlings of the land. They found the two first and brought them to us; but after a long search they could not find the others, and soe gave them up, saying the wolves must have eaten them. There were some that thought John Billington had never seen them either, but had shot them with a long bowe. Be this as it may, Mistress Winslow and the other women stripped them they had, cleaned them, spytted them, basted them, and roasted them, and thus we had fresh foule to our dinner."

I say it would have been very pleasant to have found this in some palimpsest, but if it is in the palimpsest, it has not yet been found. As the Arab proverb says, "There is news, but it has not yet come."

I have failed, in just the same way, to find a letter from that rosy-cheeked little child you see in Sargent's picture, looking out of her great wondering eyes, under her warm hood, into the desert. I overhauled a good many of the Cotton manuscripts in the British Museum (Otho and Caligula, if anybody else wants to look), and Mr. Sainsbury let me look through all the portfolios I wanted in the State Paper Office, and I am sure the letter was not there then. If anybody has found it, it has been found since I was there. If it ever is found, I should like to have it contain the following statement:—

"We got tired of playing by the fire, and so some of us ran down to the brook, and walked till we could find a place to cross it; and so came up to a meadow as large as the common place in Leyden. There was a good deal of ice upon it in some places, but in some places behind, where there were bushes, we found good store of berries growing on the ground. I filled my apron, and William took off his jerkin and made a bag of it, and we all filled it to carry up to the fire. But they were so sour, that they puckered our mouths sadly. But my mother said they were cranberries, but not like your cranberries in Lincolnshire. And, having some honey in one of the logs the men cut down, she boiled the cranberries and the honey together, and after it was cold we had it with our dinner. And besides, there were some great pompions which the men had brought with them from the first place we landed at, which were not like Cinderella's, but had long tails to them, and of these my mother and Mrs. Brewster and Mrs. Warren, made pies for dinner. We found afterwards that the Indians called these pompions, *askuta squash*."

But this letter, I am sorry to say, has not yet been found.

Whether they had roast turkey for Christmas I do not know. I do know, thanks to the recent discovery of the old Bradford manuscript, that they did have roast turkey at their first Thanksgiving. The veritable history, like so much more of it, alas! is the history of what they had not, instead of the history of what they had. Not only did they work on the day when all their countrymen played, but they had only water to drink on the day when all their countrymen drank beer. This deprivation of beer is a trial spoken of more than once; and, as lately as 1824, Mr. Everett, in his Pilgrim oration, brought it in high up in the climax of the catalogue of their hardships. How many of us in our school declamations have stood on one leg, as bidden in "Lovell's Speaker," raised the hand of the other side to an angle of forty-five degrees, as also bidden, and repeated, as also bidden, not to say compelled, the words, "I see them, escaped from these perils, pursuing their almost desperate undertaking, and landed at last, after a five-months' passage, on the ice-clad rocks of Plymouth, weak and exhausted from the voyage, poorly armed, scantily provisioned, depending on the charity of their ship-master for a draught of beer on board, drinking nothing but water on shore, without shelter, without means, surrounded by hostile tribes."

Little did these men of 1620 think that the time would come when ships would go round the world without a can of beer on board; that armies would fight through years of war without a ration of beer or of spirit, and that the builders of the Lawrences and Vinelands, the pioneer towns of a new Christian civilization, would put the condition into the title-deeds of their property that nothing should be sold there which could intoxicate the buyer. Poor fellows! they missed the beer, I am afraid, more than they did the play at Christmas; and as they had not yet learned how good water is for a steady drink, the carnal mind almost rejoices that when they got on board that Christmas night, the curmudgeon ship-master, warmed up by his Christmas jollifications, for he had no scruples, treated to beer all round, as the reader has seen. With that tankard of beer—as those who went on board filled it, passed it, and refilled it—ends the history of the first Christmas in New England.

It is a very short story, and yet it is the longest history of that Christmas that I have been able to find. I wanted to compare this celebration of Christmas, grimly intended for its desecration, with some of the celebrations which were got up with painstaking intention. But, alas, pageants leave little history, after the lights have smoked out, and the hangings have been taken away. Leaving, for the moment, King James's Christmas and Englishmen, I thought it would be a pleasant thing to study the contrast of a Christmas in the countries where they say Christmas has its most enthusiastic welcome. So I studied up the war in the Palatinate,—I went into the chronicles of Spain, where I thought they would take pains about Christmas,—I tried what the men of "la religion," the Huguenots, were doing at Rochelle, where a great assembly was gathering. But Christmas day would not appear in memoirs or annals. I tried Rome and the Pope, but he was dying, like the King of Spain, and had not, I think, much heart for pageantry. I looked in at Vienna, where they had all been terribly frightened by Bethlem Gabor, who was a great Transylvanian prince of those days, a sort of successful Kossuth, giving much hope to beleaguered Protestants farther west, who, I believe, thought for a time that he was some sort of seal or trumpet, which, however, he did not prove to be. At this moment of time he was retreating I am afraid, and at all events did not set his historiographer to work describing his Christmas festivities.

Passing by Bethlem Gabor then, and the rest, from mere failure of their chronicles to make note of this Christmas as it passed, I returned to France in my quest. Louis XIII. was at this time reigning with the assistance of Luynes, the short-lived favorite who preceded Richelieu. Or it would, perhaps, be more proper to say that Luynes was reigning under the name of Louis XIII. Louis XIII. had been spending the year in great activity, deceiving, thwarting, and undoing the Protestants of France. He had made a rapid march into their country, and had spread terror before him. He had had mass celebrated in Navarreux, where it had not been seen or heard in fifty years. With Bethlem Gabor in the ablative,—with the Palatinate quite in the vocative,—these poor Huguenots here outwitted and outgeneralled, and Brewster and Carver freezing out there in America, the Reformed Religion seems in a bad way to one looking at that Christmas. From his triumphal and almost bloodless campaign, King Louis returns to Paris, "and there," says Bassompierre, "he celebrated the *fêtes* this Christmas." So I thought I was going to find in the memoirs of some gentleman at court, or unoccupied mistress of the robes, an account of what the most Christian King was doing, while the blisters were forming on John Carver's hands, and while John Billington was, or was not, shooting wild turkeys on that eventful Christmas day.

But I reckoned without my king. For this is all a mistake, and whatever else is certain, it seems to be certain that King Louis XIII. did not keep either Christmas in Paris, either the Christmas of the Old Style, or that of the New. Such, alas, is history, dear friend! When you read in to-night's "Evening Post" that your friend Dalrymple is appointed Minister to Russia, where he has been so anxious to go, do not suppose he will make you his Secretary of Legation. Alas! no; for you will read in to-morrow's "Times" that it was all a mistake of the telegraph, and that the dispatch should have read "O'Shaughnessy," where the dispatch looked like "Dalrymple." So here, as I whetted my pencil, wetted my lips, and drove the attentive librarian at the Astor almost frantic as I sent him up stairs for you five times more, it proved that Louis XIII. did not spend Christmas in Paris, but that Bassompierre, who said so, was a vile

deceiver. Here is the truth in the *Mercure Française*,—flattering and obsequious Annual Register of those days:

"The King at the end of this year, visited the frontiers of Picardy. In
this whole journey, which lasted from the 14th of December to the 12th
of January (New Style), the weather was bad, and those in his Majesty's
suite found the roads bad." Change the style back to the way our Puritans
counted it, and observe that on the same days, the 5th of December to the
3d of January, Old Style, those in the suite of John Carver found the weather
bad and the roads worse. Let us devoutly hope that his most Christian
Majesty did not find the roads as bad as his suite did.

"And the King," continues the *Mercure*, "sent an extraordinary
Ambassador to the King of Great Britain, at London, the Marshal Cadenet"
(brother of the favorite Luynes). "He departed from Calais on Friday, the
first day of January, very well accompanied by *noblesse*. He arrived at Dover
the same evening, and did not depart from Dover until the Monday after."

Be pleased to note, dear reader, that this Monday, when this
Ambassador of a most Christian King departs from Dover, is on Monday
the 25th day of December, of Old Style, or Protestant Style, when John
Carver is learning wood-cutting, by way of encouraging the others. Let
us leave the King of France to his bad roads, and follow the fortunes of
the favorite's brother, for we must study an English Christmas after all.
We have seen the Christmas holidays of men who had hard times for the
reward of their faith in the Star of Bethlehem. Let us try the fortunes of
the most Christian King's people, as they keep their second Christmas of
the year among a Protestant people. Observe that a week after their own
Christmas of New Style, they land in Old Style England, where Christmas
has not yet begun. Here is the *Mercure Français's* account of the Christmas
holidays,—flattering and obsequious, as I said:

"Marshal Cadenet did not depart from Dover till the Monday after"
(Christmas day, O. S.). "The English Master of Ceremonies had sent
twenty carriages and three hundred horses for his suite." (If only we
could have ten of the worst of them at Plymouth! They would have drawn
our logs for us that half quarter of a mile. But we were not born in the
purple!) "He slept at Canterbury, where the Grand Seneschal of England,
well accompanied by English noblemen, received him on the part of the
King of England. Wherever he passed, the officers of the cities made
addresses to him, and offers, even ordering their own archers to march
before him and guard his lodgings. When he came to Gravesend, the Earl
of Arundel visited him on the part of the King, and led him to the Royal
barge. His whole suite entered into twenty-five other barges, painted,
hung with tapestry, and well adorned" (think of our poor, rusty shallop
there in Plymouth bay), "in which, ascending the Thames, they arrived

in London Friday the 29th December" (January 8th, N. S.). "On disembarking, the Ambassador was led by the Earl of Arundel to the palace of the late Queen, which had been superbly and magnificently arranged for him. The day was spent in visits on the part of his Majesty the King of Great Britain, of the Prince of Wales, his son, and of the ambassadors of kings and princes, residing in London." So splendidly was he entertained, that they write that on the day of his reception he had four tables, with fifty covers each, and that the Duke of Lennox, Grand Master of England, served them with magnificent order.

"The following Sunday" (which we could not spend on shore), "he was conducted to an audience by the Marquis of Buckingham," (for shame, Jamie! an audience on Sunday! what would John Knox have said to that!) "where the French and English nobility were dressed as for a great feast day. The whole audience was conducted with great respect, honor, and ceremony. The same evening, the King of Great Britain sent for the Marshal by the Marquis of Buckingham and the Duke of Lennox; and his Majesty and the Ambassador remained alone for more than two hours, without any third person hearing what they said. The following days were all receptions, banquets, visits, and hunting-parties, till the embassy departed."

That is the way history gets written by a flattering and obsequious court editor or organ at the time. That is the way, then, that the dread sovereign of John Carver and Edward Winslow spent his Christmas holidays, while they were spending theirs in beginning for him an empire. Dear old William Brewster used to be a servant of Davison's in the days of good Queen Bess. As he blows his fingers there in the twenty-foot storehouse before it is roofed, does he tell the rest sometimes of the old wassail at court, and the Christmas when the Earl of Southampton brought Will. Shakespeare in? Perhaps those things are too gay,—at all events, we have as much fuel here as they have at St. James's.

Of this precious embassy, dear reader, there is not a word, I think, in Hume, or Lingard, or the "Pictorial"—still less, if possible, in the abridgments. Would you like, perhaps, after this truly elegant account thus given by a court editor, to look behind the canvas and see the rough ends of the worsted? I always like to. It helps me to understand my morning "Advertiser" or my "Evening Post," as I read the editorial history of to-day. If you please, we will begin in the Domestic State Papers of England, which the good sense of somebody, I believe kind Sir Francis Palgrave, has had opened for you and me and the rest of us.

Here is the first notice of the embassy:

Dec. 13. Letter from Sir Robert Naunton

to Sir George Calvert. . . . "The King of France is expected at Calais. The Marshal of Cadenet is to be sent over to calumniate those of the religion (that is, the Protestants), and to propose Madme. Henriette for the Prince."

So they knew, it seems, ten days before we started, what we were coming for.

Dec. 22. John Chamberlain to Sir Dudley Carleton. "In spite of penury, there is to be a masque at Court this Christmas. The King is coming in from Theobalds to receive the French Ambassador, Marshal Cadenet, who comes with a suite of 400 or 500."

What was this masque? Could not Mr. Payne Collier find up the libretto, perhaps? Was it Faith, Valor, Hope, and Love, founding a kingdom, perhaps? Faith with a broadaxe, Valor and Hope with a two-handled saw, while Love dug post-holes and set up timbers? Or was it a less appropriate masque of King James' devising?

Dec. 25. This is our day. Francis Willisfourd, Governor of Dover Castle to Lord Zouch, Warden of the Cinque Ports. "A French Ambassador has landed with a great train. I have not fired a salute, having no instructions, and declined showing them the fortress. They are entertained as well as the town can afford."

Observe, we are a little surly. We do not like the French King very well, our own King's daughter being in such straits yonder in the Palatinate. What do these Papists here?

That is the only letter written on Christmas day in the English "Domestic Archives" for that year! Christmas is for frolic here, not for letter-writing, nor house-building, if one's houses be only built already!

But on the 27th, Wednesday, "Lord Arundel has gone to meet the French Ambassador at Gravesend." And a very pretty time it seems they had at Gravesend, when you look on the back of the embroidery. Arundel called on Cadenet at his lodgings, and Cadenet did not meet him till he came to the stair—head of his chamber-door—nor did he accompany him further when he left. But Arundel was even with him the next morning. He appointed his meeting for the return call *in the street*; and when the barges had come up to Somerset House, where the party was to stay, Arundel left the Ambassador, telling him that there were gentlemen who would show him his lodging. The King was so angry that he made Cadenet apologize. Alas for the Court of Governor John Carver on this side,—four days old to-day—if Massasoit should send us an ambassador! *We* shall have to receive him in the street, unless he likes to come into a palace without a roof! But, fortunately, he does not send till we are ready!

The Domestic Archives give another glimpse:

Dec. 30. Thomas Locke to Carleton: "The French Ambassador has arrived at Somerset House with a train so large that some of the seats at Westminster Hall had to be pulled down to make room at their audience." And in letters from the same to the same, of January 7, are accounts of entertainments given to the Ambassador at his first audience (on that Sunday), on the 4th at Parliament House, on the 6th at a masque at Whitehall, where none were allowed below the rank of a Baron—and at Lord Doncaster's entertainment—where "six thousand ounces of gold are set out as a present," says the letter, but this I do not believe. At the Hampton entertainment, and at the masque there were some disputes about precedency, says John Chamberlain in another letter. Dear John Chamberlain, where are there not such disputes? At the masque at Whitehall he says, "a Puritan was flouted and abused, which was thought unseemly, considering the state of the French Protestants." Let the Marshal come over to Gov. John Carver's court and see one of our masques there, if he wants to know about Puritans. "At Lord Doncaster's house the feast cost three thousand pounds, beside three hundred pounds worth of ambergris used in the cooking," nothing about that six thousand ounces of gold. "The Ambassador had a long private interview with the king; it is thought he proposed Mad. Henriette for the Prince. He left with a present of a rich jewel. He requested liberation of all the imprisoned priests in the three kingdoms, but the answer is not yet given."

By the eleventh of January the embassy had gone, and Thomas Locke says Cadenet "received a round answer about the Protestants." Let us hope it was so, for it was nearly the last, as it was. Thomas Murray writes that he "proposed a match with France,—a confederation against Spanish power, and asked his Majesty to abandon the rebellious princes,—but he refused unless they might have toleration." The Ambassador was followed to Rochester for the debts of some of his train,—but got well home to Paris and New Style.

And so he vanishes from English history.

His king made him Duke of Chaulnes and Peer of France, but his brother, the favorite died soon after, either of a purple fever or of a broken heart, and neither of them need trouble us more.

At the moment the whole embassy seemed a failure in England,—and so it is spoken of by all the English writers of the time whom I have seen. "There is a flaunting French Ambassador come over lately," says Howel, "and I believe his errand is naught else but compliment. . . . He had an audience two days since, where he, with his train of ruffling long-haired Monsieurs, carried himself in such a light garb, that after the audience the king asked my Lord Keeper Bacon what he thought of the French Ambassador. He answered, that he was a tall, proper man. 'Aye,' his Majesty replied, 'but what think you of his head-piece? Is he a proper man for the office of an ambassador?' 'Sir,' said Bacon, 'tall men are like houses of four or five stories, wherein commonly the uppermost room is worst furnished.'"

Hard, this, on us poor six-footers. One need not turn to the biography after this, to guess that the philosopher was five feet four.

I think there was a breeze, and a cold one, all the time, between the embassy and the English courtiers. I could tell you a good many stories to show this, but I would give them all for one anecdote of what Edward Winslow said to Madam Carver on Christmas evening. They thought it all naught because they did not know what would come of it. We do know.

And I wish you to observe, all the time, beloved reader, whom I press to my heart for your steadiness in perusing so far, and to whom I would give a jewel had I one worthy to give, in token of my consideration (how you would like a Royalston beryl or an Attleboro topaz).*

I wish you to observe, I say, that on the Christmas tide, when the Forefathers began New England, Charles and Henrietta were first proposed to each other for that fatal union. Charles, who was to be Charles the First, and Henrietta, who was to be mother of Charles the Second, and James the Second. So this was the time, when were first proposed all the precious intrigues and devisings, which led to Charles the Second, James the Second, James the Third, so called, and our poor friend the Pretender. Civil War—Revolution—1715—1745—Preston-Pans, Falkirk and Culloden—all are in the dispatches Cadenet carries ashore at Dover, while we are hewing our timbers at the side of the brook at Plymouth, and making our contribution to Protestant America.

On the one side Christmas is celebrated by fifty outcasts chopping wood for their fires—and out of the celebration springs an empire. On the other side it is celebrated by the *noblesse* of two nations and the pomp of two courts. And out of the celebration spring two civil wars, the execution of one king and the exile of another, the downfall twice repeated of the royal house, which came to the English throne under fairer auspices than ever. The whole as we look at it is the tale of ruin. Those are the only two Christmas celebrations of that year that I have found anywhere written down!

You will not misunderstand the moral, dear reader, if, indeed, you exist; if at this point there be any reader beside him who corrects the proof! Sublime thought of the solemn silence in which these words may be spoken! You will not misunderstand the moral. It is not that it is better to work on Christmas than to play. It is not that masques turn out ill, and that those who will not celebrate the great anniversaries turn out well. God forbid!

It is that these men builded better than they knew, because they did with all their heart and all their soul the best thing that they knew. They loved

* Mrs. Hemans says they did not seek "bright jewels of the mine," which was fortunate, as they would not have found them. Attleboro is near Plymouth Rock, but its jewels are not from mines. The beryls of Royalston are, but they are far away. Other good mined jewels, I think, New England has none. Her garnets are poor, and I have yet seen no good amethysts.

Christ and feared God, and on Christmas day did their best to express the love and the fear. And King James and Cadenet,—did they love Christ and fear God? I do not know. But I do not believe, nor do you, that the masque of the one, or the embassy of the other, expressed the love, or the hope, or the faith of either!

So it was that John Carver and his men, trying to avoid the celebration of the day, built better than they knew indeed, and, in their faith, laid a corner-stone for an empire.

And James and Cadenet trying to serve themselves—forgetful of the spirit of the day, as they pretended to honor it—were so successful that they destroyed a dynasty.

There is moral enough for our truer Christmas holidays as 1867 leads in the new-born sister.

The End

www.ingramcontent.com/pod-product-compliance
Lightning Source LLC
Chambersburg PA
CBHW030535130626
46552CB00006B/2276